SHEILA SPENCER-SMITH

◆

SHEARWATER COVE

Complete and Unabridged

LINFORD
Leicester

First published in Great Britain in 2015

First Linford Edition
published 2017

A catalogue record for this book is available
from the British Library.

ISBN 978–1–4448–3151–1

Published by
F. A. Thorpe (Publishing)
Anstey, Leicestershire

Set by Words & Graphics Ltd.
Anstey, Leicestershire
Printed and bound in Great Britain by
T. J. International Ltd., Padstow, Cornwall

This book is printed on acid-free paper

1

There was no doubt that Miranda's disappearance had come at just the right time. Lucy Cameron, her normal quick sympathy dormant for a moment, had rejoiced when she heard that her cousin's wife had left the islands. How selfish, how unfeeling, was that?

In shame, Lucy looked down at her feet and saw the spider crawling across the kitchen floor. It would serve her right if a whole legion of them emerged from the woodwork. She grabbed her *Scillonian* ferry ticket and slid it underneath the creature. The next instant it was outside and she had slammed the back door behind it.

'Phew!'

She leant against the draining board in her Truro flat to recover from her fearless act. But she wasn't as brave as poor Cousin Josh. His decision to carry on the business without Miranda would have been a hard one, and she admired him for it.

She hadn't asked why his wife had left when he phoned to ask if she could possibly come and help out. By a miracle, there were at least two weeks' leave from the bookshop owing to her — more, if what her elderly employer had admitted was true. He had looked up, a little bleary-eyed, from close study of his archaeological tome when she asked about leave. She had felt a pang of sympathy for him, but her chief concern must be Josh's obvious unhappiness and need.

For the last year or two he had refused to talk about his new wife's ban on any of his relations continuing to visit Polwhenna every summer. Lucy had felt this keenly at the time but had come to accept it. Josh was happy with his lovely Miranda, and that was that.

But now things were different.

The honking of her taxi was the signal she was waiting for. She took a last look round, heaved up her suitcase and hand luggage, and headed outside.

The early-morning air was full of shrieking gulls when her train arrived in Penzance. Sunlight reflected off the huge luggage containers as they were fork-lifted away along the quay to be loaded on board the *Scillonian*. Lucy wheeled her suitcase over the cobbles with difficulty to where the men were waiting to take it from her. She had been careful to write only her name on the luggage label so that it wouldn't be delivered automatically to Polwhenna. Josh had promised to collect it when he met her from the *Scillonian*.

She handed in the boarding card she had collected at the kiosk, and then was aware of a sudden commotion as a late passenger joined the queue. He was close behind her as she found a seat on the top deck, which was filling up fast. Men on the quay were already in position at the bollards, ready to slip off the massive ropes to free the vessel.

The latecomer sank down in the seat

opposite her and let out a long breath. His hair was the colour of damp autumn leaves, a deep rich colour that made Lucy think of bright October afternoons and the deep red of the embers of fragrant wood fires.

She smiled. 'You might have had to swim for it,' she said.

The amused expression in his eyes seemed to deepen. 'You're making fun of me.'

'I never make fun of strange men.'

'Only of familiar ones?'

'Not even those.'

'If you say so.' His voice was slightly husky. Tom's had been higher-pitched and his hair much darker, but the likeness was uncanny. 'I can't sit here for long getting over the stress of that last-minute dash,' he said. 'I have work to do.' He sprang up, scattering a handful of leaflets at Lucy's feet. 'Here, take one of these,' he said as he gathered them up. 'People like to know what's out there at sea.'

'You do this on a regular basis?'

'Not the scattering of them in such abandon, I have to admit. I don't know what's got into me.' She laughed. He stood up straight and then gave a mock bow. 'Matt Henderson, reliable and informative and on the ball at all times, except today. There's usually one of us at least on board each trip. My sister's here somewhere, on the lower deck I expect. Scientific research, you see, for the records. We always let the passengers know if we spot something in case they're interested.'

'And are they?'

'You'd be surprised.'

'So what d'you hope to see today?'

'Dolphins or porpoise, if we're lucky and the conditions are right.' He had a slow way of talking, as if he had given the matter deep thought. Lucy liked that.

'Or man-eating sharks,' she suggested. 'And blue whales.'

His lips curved into a smile. 'Knowledgeable about wildlife, are you?'

'My father's a marine biologist. Mum

was keen on seals. I'm looking forward to beaches full of them.'

He raised his eyebrows. 'At this time of the year?'

'Why not?'

'Not so knowledgeable after all, then.'

Well, no, she thought as he moved away. Except to have learned from an early age that all wildlife was sacred, even spiders.

Soon Penzance was slipping away behind them in the breezy morning sunshine. As the *Scillonian* turned to follow the Cornish coast, the wind strengthened and sent some of her fellow passengers scuttling down below to the comfort of the cabin. But Lucy revelled in the fierce salty air on her face and the movement of the vessel as they journeyed on to the islands somewhere in the invisible distance.

Leaning back, she closed her eyes for a moment, thinking of Josh and his welcome invitation that had come at just the right time. She needed to get away after her split with Tom, mutual though it was, and she couldn't think of anywhere she would rather be than those magical islands she hadn't seen for a long time.

Voices round her rose and fell. They sounded far away at first, and then nearer. She opened her eyes. She was conscious now of a sudden stir, and saw a group of people staring at something in the sea some distance behind them. She stood up for a better view of the churning water as a flock of gannets swooped and plummeted, marvelling at the wings folded like arrowheads and the sheer elegance of the diving birds. Once they were out of sight, the group of onlookers dispersed. Matt Henderson wasn't among them imparting information, she noticed. Perhaps gannets were too common and not worthy of mention.

He hadn't seemed at all put out by her comments as he moved on among the family groups of holiday-makers, head and shoulders above the rest. He was used to it, probably. People on holiday were often like that, totally relaxed and ready to smile and joke about anything. It was like the feeling she had now, suspended between two worlds.

She glanced at the leaflet in her hand, holding it tightly so it wouldn't be snatched away by a gust of wind. It explained a little of what he was doing aboard the *Scillonian* and also gave an overview of some weekly talks on wildlife in the main island's small town of Hugh Town. Manx Shearwaters seemed to feature a lot, particularly the serious problems with their nesting sites.

Wild croquet parties on the lawn and barbecues getting out of hand were the only wildlife she was likely to encounter in the next week or two. Josh would be coping with the important stuff because Miranda had left him well and truly in it.

So enter Lucy, full of zeal and ready to do her bit.

2

Polwhenna stood in its acre of garden looking strangely the same as the last time Lucy had seen it. That was before Mum died and they had come over to the islands to help celebrate Uncle Eric's eightieth birthday. That was five years ago now, just as she was starting work at Good Reads. The only difference she could see was the lack of hanging baskets that Uncle Eric, Josh's late father, had filled with an unusual mixture of lobelia and nasturtium plants. The orange and yellow flowers mingled with the blue of the lobelia in unexpected splendour.

'The hanging baskets have gone,' Lucy said, disappointed.

'Miranda didn't like them so she got rid of them,' Josh told her as he got out of the car and lifted Lucy's suitcase out for her. 'She said they were a job we could do without. She was right, as she was about most things.'

But not about leaving him so suddenly, Lucy thought.

Josh looked just the same, which was surprising after all had been through. He was wearing his usual long shorts, and his fair hair was cut short. Even in his old grey polo shirt, he had been easy for Lucy to pick out among the people on the quay because of the way he lounged against the wall waiting for her to appear. Typically laid-back at all times, that was Josh. It was a wonder that he had turned up in time to meet the *Scillonian*, but there he was, and she was pleased to see him.

'All set then?' he had said.

'All set.'

'My vehicle's back there. Here, let me take your case.' It was on wheels, but he heaved it up as if it weighed no more than a bag of grass clippings.

The cobbled quay was just as Lucy remembered it, with the boats tied up alongside waiting for their afternoon passengers for the off islands, everyone happy and glad to be there, the sun shining.

Traffic blocked the narrow main street but no one seemed to mind. Josh sat at the wheel, smiling a little as he waited for it to clear. And then they were away, travelling out of town past a silver beach Lucy remembered and up the road that led to the north of the island and Polwhenna. She was aware all the time that the sea was close, even though she couldn't see it now. There was something about the clearness of the air and the light. She was glad to be back.

Josh put her case down near the front porch and indicated that she should follow him on along the path that she knew led round to the back of the property. 'There's somewhere I want to show you first, Lucy.'

The pride in his voice was unmistakable, and she smiled to hear it. Josh showing enthusiasm for something! Here was a change she hadn't expected.

They emerged through a stone archway of sweet-scented roses onto the wide lawn that stretched invitingly to a wide bed of shrubs backed by a tall hedge that hadn't been there before. And there had been no small dwelling overlooking the lawn either, or none that Lucy could remember as being habitable.

Josh stopped. 'Surprised?'

'I'll say.'

'This is what I want you to see, Lucy. Secret Haven, we call it.'

'But this building must have been here when I came before,' she said.

'One of the outhouses. Don't you remember, Lucy? We used this one to store stuff we didn't need. Some months ago we took the decision to convert it. Or rather, Miranda did. Take a look inside. The door's unlocked.'

She went in. The place looked surprisingly spacious and light, even though the floor wasn't yet laid. She could see the potential at once. The wall facing the door was painted in soft grey, but the one at right angles to it was a slightly different tone. Lucy checked again to make sure. Could it be the light from the spacious windows making the difference? But no, she was sure it wasn't. What was strange was that there didn't seem to be enough of a contrast in tones to make a point.

'Miranda's colour schemes, of course,' Josh said. He shrugged in a deprecating way and the expression on his face softened. 'A real gift for interior decoration, and brilliant ideas.'

'It's a beautiful place.'

'You like it?' He smiled, obviously pleased.

'And yet she left it?'

'And me.'

'Josh, I'm so sorry.' Lucy emerged into the sunlight, blinking. 'You had absolutely no idea?'

'She texted me when she was on the train in Penzance. She said it was all over.'

'And she's not coming back?'

'She said that I must have realised.'

'And you hadn't?'

'Well, no.'

'I see.'

'Someone saw them going on board the *Scillonian*.'

'And you didn't want to go after her?'

He shrugged. 'What would have been the point? Miranda was a free agent.'

'But you could have.'

'Too late,' he said sadly. 'Too late.'

Lucy supposed it was, if Miranda hadn't told him where she was going. She wanted to ask if he had texted her back and tried to phone, but it was none of her business, and obviously painful for him to talk about.

Josh closed the door behind them. Out here in the sunny garden, the birdsong seemed loud. 'I'd forgotten what a haven for wildlife this place is,' Lucy said.

Josh nodded, other things obviously on his mind as they began to walk back to the house. 'Your room's on the top floor, Lucy. One of the students has got it ready for you. We've got two of them

14

here for a few weeks — Australians. Great cooks, and they're happy to see to the occasional evening meal. Did I tell you — they got here yesterday. Free accommodation for helping out here every morning.'

This was another surprise, and a pleasant one. They went into the house.

'Come down when you've settled,' Josh said. 'There's lunch waiting for you. Cold, so take your time.'

But Lucy didn't need to get settled and her unpacking could wait. A quick look round her smallish room, with its sloping ceiling and deep-set window overlooking the garden at the back, was enough for the time being. She wanted to meet the two students and find out what her duties were to be. And what was more, she was hungry.

There was no one in the kitchen. The wooden table was laden with a selection of salads and cold meat, and there was a breadboard with two loaves and a pat of butter in a dish on it.

'We generally eat outside when the

weather's good,' Josh said as he came in behind her. 'This spread is in your honour, I think. They seem to have overdone it a bit. Help yourself.'

Afterwards they sat outside at the picnic table to drink their coffee. Here the high hedges round a smaller lawn provided enough shade on this hot day to be pleasant. Bees murmured among the lavender bush and the honeysuckle. Lucy felt her eyelids begin to droop.

'Tired?' said Josh.

She jerked herself upright. 'Not really.'

'Was it hectic for you packing to come, and leaving the bookshop in good order?'

'There wasn't a lot to do,' she said, and sighed. She hadn't meant to voice her anxiety about her elderly employer and the lack of business, but there was something about Josh that invited confidences. She hesitated. No, she must keep it to herself. Josh had enough worries without her unloading her concerns.

'I'd like to phone my boss, Angus, to say I'm here in one piece,' she said. 'He seemed to think that travelling here on my own might be a bit beyond me.'

Josh smiled. He finished the last of his coffee and stood up. 'Go ahead while I see to the washing up. Then I'll show you round the place and explain a few things.'

'But I can't let you — '

His smile was sweet as he picked up the empty mugs. 'I'm a dab hand at washing the dishes, Lucy.'

She left a message on the bookshop's answerphone, smiling a little as she imagined Angus taking too long to push his book aside and reach the phone. He would most likely have been engrossed in one of his favourite works about the Iron Age, poring closely over the small print with his glasses balanced on the end of his nose. When she had told him of Josh's cry for help, he had looked over them with such concern that she had been filled with affection for this gentle man who cared about her well-being. He was like a grandfather to her.

'My dear Lucy,' he had said, 'of course you must consider you cousin's needs. And, my dear girl, take as long away as you like.'

His kindness to her in spite of his deep concern about his failing business was almost overwhelming. Coping with emotion of any sort wasn't his strong point, and so she had thanked him for his kindness and then turned away so that he wouldn't see the tears in her eyes.

There were four letting properties at Polwhenna, and Josh told her that they had all been recently modernised. He didn't say so, but obviously Miranda had seen to all that. From the outside they looked attractively old and established, and had always been referred to as cottages.

'You'll see the inside of two of them tomorrow at changeover,' Josh said. 'For the other two, the changeover's on Tuesday. It makes life easier for us.'

Lucy nodded in approval, wanting to ask if that was Miranda's idea too. 'Where is everybody?' she said instead.

'We've got four couples in this week and they like to get out and about. Unless there's anyone by the pool.'

'A swimming pool?'

'Miranda said we needed one. Come on, I'll show you.'

The hedges were high enough for privacy, but surrounding the large pool was a huge area of paving edged with flowerbeds. The colourful cushions on the cane sunbeds gave a luxurious touch. A spacious suntrap, perfect!

In the pool were two girls. 'Tanya, Annie!' Josh called. One of the girls turned a startled face to him and made for the side of the pool to clamber out. The other carried on swimming with powerful strokes that ate up the distance from one end to the other in seconds. Then she too got out, shook herself and squared her shoulders.

'Lucy, this is Tanya,' Josh said, frowning. He turned to the other girl

19

and smiled. 'And Annie. The rules are quite clear, Tanya. The pool is for guests only in the daytime.'

'So where are they all then?'

'Early morning, later in the evening. That's the time for the staff.' The tone of his voice was surprisingly mild.

'Staff!' Tanya spat out.

'Sorry, Josh,' the other girl, Annie, said. 'It was just . . . well, it just looked really grouse.'

'Grouse?'

'Good,' Tanya explained. 'Too right it did.'

Lucy could agree with that, but she could see Josh's point. Their guests must feel special. She was pleased that he insisted on that and made it plain from the start. Good for him. She looked from one girl to the other. At first sight she had thought Polwhenna a haven of tranquillity, but now with just this hint of hostility she wasn't so sure.

Tanya snatched up her towel from the low wall where she had left it, slipped her feet into a pair of flowery flip-flops, and went stalking off. With a startled look at Lucy, Annie followed.

Josh was silent for a moment. Then he shrugged and turned to Lucy. He pointed to another gap in the hedge on the other side of the pool. 'The barbecue area's through there. Guests are at liberty to use it when they like as long as they leave it in good order.'

'So cleaning it won't be one of my jobs?'

'You'll be the overall inspector of the property, keeping things running smoothly.'

'Inspector? Tanya won't think much of that.'

'No?'

'Call me your assistant, Josh. Why don't you write down all the things that need doing at Polwhenna, and we'll decide which will be my responsibilities?'

'Good plan,' said Josh. 'I should have thought of it. Miranda — '

'Lucy.'

He blinked. 'Yes, Lucy. Let's do that then.'

'I'll get unpacked while you get started on it. Fifteen minutes?'

'Fifteen minutes.'

Lucy was pleased to see that Josh looked more cheerful now, glad that she was being bossy. So that was the way it was going to have to be, if it was what he wanted.

'See you then,' he said.

She allowed him twenty minutes just to make sure. She found him at the picnic table on their private patio outside the kitchen. He had a pad in front of him and a pen stuck behind one ear. 'It's tricky,' he said as she sat down opposite him and leant forward to read his list. 'I forgot you could read upside down.' He removed his pencil and tapped it on the table.

'One of my few talents.'

He raised his eyebrows. 'Few?'

'You haven't got many things written on the list yet.'

'I'm a bit stuck.'

'You said the girls see to the cleaning of the flats when the clients leave?'

'Cottages.'

'Sorry. Cottages.'

'The cleaning? That's right, among other things.'

'So what do you do?'

He gave one of his expressive shrugs. 'This and that.'

'You don't know?'

'Wash the breakfast things. Hang about a bit to say farewell when the guests leave on a Saturday and then get started on the lawns for the weekly cut. Trim a few shrubs. Get stuck in on the vegetable garden. Answer emails. Write receipts for deposits when the post comes and deal with queries, fill in the booking chart. Photocopy cheques for the record, too. Get the washing machine on. Be around to welcome the new arrivals and show them round a bit. Check the vacant cottages for necessary repairs and carry them out. Order supplies.'

'By phone? Online?'

'Whatever.'

Lucy took the list from him, and wrote each new item down as he spoke. There were more too, of course; a mixture of jobs that meant Josh was busy moving from one to the other, going back and forth from inside to out. Not good. 'And what do the girls do when the cleaning's done?'

Josh was vague. 'They'll cook tea for us today, and then they're planning to go down to town for the evening and see what's what.'

'How will they get down there?'

'I'll drive them down. Why don't you go too?'

'I was thinking I'd take a walk down to the beach. For old times' sake, you know.'

'And you must make sure you take time off every day yourself, Lucy.'

'You too, Josh. So let's divide the work amongst us all and write down the job descriptions, and then I'll type them out.'

'Great.'

The task was enjoyable because they were out in the sunshine doing something useful. Josh seemed to feel the same, and agreed that the lists for Lucy and the girls should be displayed on the cork noticeboard in the kitchen.

When she had done that, Lucy stood back to see how it looked just as Tanya came into the room. She scrutinised Lucy's handiwork. 'Good on ya,' she said. Her tone was begrudging, as if forced to admit it against her will. 'But our list isn't straight. I like things right.' She adjusted it, her tongue between her lips, and then picked up the cookery book from the dresser and turned to go. 'There's some sort of open event at the farm on Sunday, the place round the corner. Will you be going to that?'

'It depends what other plans Josh has,' Lucy said.

'Oh he'll be there too,' Tanya said, her voice bitter. 'The locals all stick together, you know. That's what Josh told us. Support each other whenever they can.'

'Aren't you happy here, Tanya?' Lucy said in surprise.

'Happy? What's that got to do with it? Josh ought to be hard at it here, getting that other place ready for letting. He needs the money.'

Lucy took a quick intake of breath. This was a bit of an assumption coming from a young employee, and a newly arrived temporary one at that. True, perhaps, but it wasn't Tanya's place to comment.

★ ★ ★

The poster that the young boy was pinning to the noticeboard on the farmyard wall looked interesting. He was standing on the top rung of a stepladder, banging in stout pins to hold it in position. Lucy paused for a closer look at the bold black print on the yellow background. 'That'll be hard to for anyone to miss,' she said.

The boy turned to grin at her, his dark hair sticking up in peaks. His wiry frame looked perfectly balanced, but she was perturbed by the rocking of the steps and relieved when he jumped down.

'That's the idea,' he said. 'Hope to see you here.'

'Farm Open Event,' Lucy read out loud. 'Local produce, stalls, games, competitions, tractor rides, cream teas. Sounds good. You live here?'

'Son of the house. Carl Birkett.'

'Lucy Hammond.'

'Josh's cousin. Welcome to Scilly.'

'I feel welcome already.'

He nodded. 'That's what we like to hear.'

He said it so simply and in such a mature way that Lucy was touched. 'And of course I'm coming on Sunday,' she said. 'It's my first social occasion here, so it had better be good.'

'It's for a good cause — the Isles of Scilly Seabird Recovery Project.'

Lucy smiled. 'Then it's bound to be.'

Carl gave his notice a last critical look, and Lucy went on her way down the rutted track that led between flowery banks to the sea. She had known what to expect, but the sudden view of Shearwater Cove, its sandy beach curved on either side by grassy banks, still took her breath away. The breezy air felt good too, and she took huge breaths of it just as she used to do when she spent happy hours here as a child trying to identify the different seabirds and remember their names. There were plenty of birds this evening — diving, soaring, winging their way across the azure sky; some uttering raucous calls, others running on thin fussy legs across the expanse of sand by the water's edge.

The tide was in, and so the line of rocks Lucy knew were there were invisible beneath the rippling water. The island that wasn't really an island looked as if there was always a strip of water dividing it from the beach. She would come down here earlier another

28

time when the tide was low, scramble across to reach it, and make her way up through the mass of undergrowth to the highest part. From there she would have an even better view of the other islands across the water that were now sleeping in the early evening haze.

She walked a little way, then pulled off her trainers so she could feel the softness of the sand beneath her feet.

3

Lucy felt sad saying goodbye to the two couples leaving the next day, even though she had hardly known them in the short time she had been there. Hugs and kisses all round and promises to return couldn't be bad.

Then the work started. She found that collecting the washing from each property to sort out in the house gave her a good excuse to keep out of the way while the girls got started on the cleaning. They both worked well because Tanya, taking the lead, had decided they should take one cottage each to cut down the chatting time. By the time Lucy had got the first load of washing in the machine and returned with fresh bedding and towels, she found that Tanya had finished both bedrooms in her cottage, Tamarisk, while Annie, with only one bedroom to clean in Pear Tree, had started on the kitchen. The background hum of the lawnmower could be heard all morning, as Josh had a lot of grass to cut around the property. It didn't quite drown out the sound of the birdsong, though, and Lucy paused every now and again to listen to it.

Annie set their simple lunch on the worktop in the kitchen. Afterwards, Josh suggested that Lucy familiarise herself with the computer during the afternoon. She could deal with any enquiries that needed attention. 'The computer work was Miranda's department,' he said.

'So what are you going to do, Josh?' Tanya said in a challenging way. He looked taken aback.

Annie stood up and carried her plate across to the sink. 'No worries,' she said. 'There's plenty else for Josh to see to, Tanya.'

'Oh rack off, Annie. What do you know?'

'You could study his list up there on the wall,' Lucy said. 'Learn it by heart, why don't you?'

Tanya glared at her. She said no more, but gulped down the last of her tea and stalked out of the room.

Josh shot Lucy a grateful look. He must be missing Miranda, who clearly wouldn't have stood for any nonsense like this, Lucy thought — any more than she would herself once they had all got settled in. Early days yet.

She spent a profitable afternoon up in the study on the first floor. This was a small dark room at the front of the house that overlooked the short drive. On the walls were framed certificates of various awards for catering and so on. She was intrigued by the photograph of a young Josh holding a fishing rod and staring at the camera as if annoyed at being forced to pose when his mind was on other things. It seemed a strange thing to have hanging here.

Lucy opened a window to let in some

fresh air. The room could do with light paint on the walls and some cheerful prints on display. A more comfortable-looking chair in front of the computer on a table that was far too large for the room would be good too.

She switched the computer on. Miranda had done a good job, and the booking folder in the document marked 'Polwhenna' was easy to locate. In it were the details of everyone who had stayed in the past year, as well as a section for future guests. Two new bookings for later in the season were easily dealt with online.

Beside the computer Lucy found a thick file, obviously a spare copy of the ones left in the cottages containing useful information for their guests to study. She carried it downstairs and sat at the picnic table outside the kitchen to browse. Bees hummed in the flowerbed nearby.

★　★　★

Lucy enjoyed the happy atmosphere at the farm next door on Sunday afternoon, wandering about in the sunshine among the games stalls that had been set up in the yard, watching people throwing hoops over pegs and guessing the number of narcissus bulbs in a sack. She had the impression that she had gone back in time to when everything was innocent and happy.

'I saw you on the *Scillonian* on Friday. I was dishing out leaflets, helping Matt.'

Lucy smiled at the friendly girl who appeared at her side. Her auburn hair was tied back in a thick plait. She tossed it back over one shoulder and didn't seem to notice when it flopped back again.

'Did you have a good response?' Lucy asked.

'Brilliant, as always. Lots of interest.'

'Great. I'm staying at Polwhenna, helping out where I can.'

The girl's face lit up. 'Then you're Lucy?'

'That's me. But how did you . . . ?'

'Josh said you were coming. I'm Penny, by the way.'

'And Matt?'

'My big brother — Matthew Henderson, supporter of the seabird recovery project on Scilly.'

'And that's the chosen good cause to benefit from this afternoon?'

'Of course. And that's why we were on board the *Scillonian*, stirring up as much interest among the visitors as we could.' Penny's cheerful face softened for a moment. 'Mum and Dad are glad to have Matt home for a bit working on the project over here. Not that we see much of him. He's been over on St Agnes most days.'

'Sounds interesting.'

'Oh it is. There's a lot involved, and he — ' She was interrupted by the roar of a tractor engine starting up. 'That's been got ready for me,' she said. 'I've got to go now. Fancy a tractor ride?'

Lucy laughed. 'Why not?'

'A pound a time for a good cause,

and cheap at the price.'

Others thought so too, and there was a lot of jostling among the children as they climbed up into the front of the trailer. Lucy was content to sit at the back squashed in beside a young boy and a large man in a purple T-shirt. A loud cheer went up as they set off.

Lucy leaned back and listened to the shrieks and laughter as the vehicle rattled its way down the uneven track towards the sea. This was an incredible thing for her to be doing; and what was more, she was enjoying it. Josh had insisted that she come to the open day, just as Tanya had said he would, assuring her that she would have a good time.

She looked at Penny, who was driving the vehicle as if she thought it was the best thing in the world to be doing on a sunny Sunday afternoon. Suddenly she stopped and switched off the engine. 'Bulb fields,' she shouted back to her passengers. 'They picked the last flowers for market in March.' The long grass in the small fields was dotted with wildflowers now, yellow and white.

'You don't see many fields like that these days,' the man next to Lucy said. 'That's why we're here.'

Lucy smiled at him as they set off again. 'Do you come every year?'

'Oh aye. Wouldn't miss it, and neither would the wife. And now there's the lad.'

The young boy on the other side of him looked anything but happy, sitting there in silence and looking down at his clenched hands. His father appeared not to notice.

On they went again, swerving into another field where an even rougher track led across to join another better one. And now they were travelling between high honeysuckle hedges away from the sea and back to the farmyard.

'Everyone out,' Penny ordered in a ringing tone.

The next lot who were waiting clambered in and Penny was off again, waving to Lucy as the tractor and trailer lumbered off. She shouted something that sounded like 'See you later', but that seemed unlikely, for it appeared that she would be busy for the rest of the afternoon.

Lucy wandered into the dim interior of the hay-scented barn, where she found more stalls that mainly sold fresh produce. One was stacked with home-made strawberry jam and marmalade. She bought a jar of each and placed them in her shoulder bag. Then she made her way back outside, wondering if she could possibly guess how many bulbs were in the sack without being wildly wrong. Too risky, she thought, contemplating it with her head held a little to one side.

She moved away and then saw an outside stall she had missed on her way in, probably because there were people clustered round it at the time looking at the posters depicting charts of seabirds. She picked up a leaflet.

'That's for one of the wildlife trips to the Eastern Isles,' a voice said.

'Oh,' she said in sudden recognition of the tall man in the stall. 'You gave me a leaflet on the boat.'

He looked pleased at being recognised, though with his looks he must surely have been used to it. Tom always expected it anyway, and was unhappy for hours if he thought he had been ignored.

'I didn't see you over there at first,' Lucy said.

'No?'

'Oh, I didn't mean . . . ' What hadn't she meant? She cleared her throat. 'Matt, isn't it? Your sister said. I've just been having a tractor ride.'

His face lit up as he smiled. 'Penny's in her element driving that thing. She only gets the chance once a year.'

'So she's making the most of it?'

'As she does with everything.'

Lucy smiled. She wanted to ask if he made the most of everything too, but at once realised that the brother and sister were quite different from each other even though they had the same colour hair and were both tall. Matt was more reserved than Penny, with a calm assurance about him that hinted of hidden strengths. Lucy had the feeling that once he put his mind to something, nothing would shift it.

She looked down at the leaflet in her hand, studying a map of the islands and looking to see how far the Eastern Isles were from St Mary's, then jumped as a plop of rain fell on it. The next moment a sudden torrent came hammering down. She leapt to help Matt gather his paperwork into an untidy heap and bundle it into boxes to carry into the shelter of the barn. Water streamed down her face, and she wiped it off with a handful of tissues, then looked round for somewhere to put them.

'Let me,' Matt said, taking them from her and pushing them into an overflowing bin.

Others had crowded in for shelter too, and the place was a heaving mass of bodies laughing and shouting above the clatter of rain on the roof.

'It won't last long,' Matt murmured in Lucy's ear.

He was right. The next moment, it seemed, the rain stopped. The barn emptied except for the stallholders. 'I won't set up out here again,' Matt said, rubbing his damp face. 'Thanks for your help, Lucy. I think that deserves a reward, don't you? How about an ice cream?'

She backed away from him. 'Oh no, I don't — '

'You don't like ice cream?' He sounded surprised. From his wet hair, a drop of rain water dribbled down the side of his face. He flicked it away.

'It's not that. It's . . . ' She broke off. An ice cream, for goodness sake — what harm was there in that? Even if she had resolved not to get close to anyone else after Tom. 'Well yes, thank you,' she said, flushing a little. 'I'd like that.'

They made their choice, and Lucy watched with interest at the generous amount that was squashed into the cornets, making them seem top-heavy as she and Matt carried them outside. The rain had left everything glistening as the sun emerged from the clouds, but the chairs at the tables were far too wet to sit on.

'Over here,' Matt said, indicating a pile of logs by the far wall. He moved off the top ones and they perched on the drier ones beneath, Lucy as far away from him as she could manage without appearing standoffish.

'We'll dry off a bit here anyway,' he said, stretching his legs out in front of him.

Lucy licked her ice cream. 'I'm glad I chose the honey and cream one.'

'Your favourite?'

'The first time I've tried it. And the first time I've sat on a pile of logs to eat one too.'

'Always a first time for everything.'

'Do you often get sudden downpours like that?'

'Sometimes. And sudden bursts of

hot sunshine like now. Everyone will soon dry off.'

Lucy looked around her and saw that what he said was true; no one seemed at all bothered. Most were shaking umbrellas or slipping their arms out of waterproofs. But one person looked as if she'd been dunked in the nearby pond as she came towards them, smiling.

'Penny!' Lucy exclaimed.

'I know. I got caught.' She pulled loose her pigtail, and her released hair flew around her face in a mass of raindrops. Her jeans were soaked, and her T-shirt looked as if it needed wringing out.

Matt finishing his ice cream. 'You'll have to get changed,' he said calmly.

'Is that all you can say?'

'They'll let you dry out at the house.'

'A bit of dampness won't hurt me.'

'It might put your passengers off though,' said Lucy. 'Come back with me, why don't you? I can lend you something.'

'To Polwhenna?'

'Just round the corner.'

'And I'll get to see round the place?'

'If that's what you'd like.'

'My sister's nothing if not nosy,' said Matt.

'Curious,' said Penny. 'That's all. I've never had the chance before.'

Josh was there when they arrived. Penny grinned cheerfully at him, with her loose hair dripping round her face. He met them in the doorway and stood aside for them to enter the house. 'So what have we here, a drowned rat?'

'Don't talk about rats,' Penny said darkly. 'You know what Matt's like. I've been hearing nothing else for weeks.'

'So how's the work going over there?'

'Don't ask me. I've had it up to here.'

Lucy looked from one to the other, perplexed. Seeing it, Penny laughed. 'Sorry. This must sound odd to you, Lucy. I'll give you the lowdown when I've got out of these wet things.'

'And into some of my dry ones,' said Lucy.

'With a shower in between no doubt,' said Josh. 'There's plenty of hot water.'

Twenty minutes later, Penny emerged from Lucy's en-suite, towelling her hair. 'That's better.'

'Use my comb,' Lucy said. 'It's by my bed.'

'Thanks.'

Penny made such an anguished face as she drew it through her mop of hair that Lucy couldn't help laughing.

'It's all right for you.' Penny's dancing eyes belied her aggrieved tone. 'Your hair is neat and pretty, Lucy, curling just a bit at the ends. Blonde too. Some people have all the luck.'

Lucy flushed a little, remembering Tom's criticism of her style being too boring. He had wanted her to cut it really short and highlight it with streaks of white for a more modern look, and complained when she had laughed at him. Modern? Clownish, more like.

She was glad to see that her jeans and T-shirt looked good on her new friend — in fact better than Penny's own clothes, because she had dressed in some old and rough things to drive the tractor. 'Don't you have to be getting back, Penny?' she asked.

'No more tractor rides this afternoon, more's the pity.'

'In that case I'll put the kettle on. Coffee?'

'You bet.'

Penny threw herself into the armchair by the table in the window and watched as Lucy set about providing it. 'It's not a bad room,' she said.

'That's what I thought when I first saw it.'

'I've got a tiny attic room at our place. All the rest are for our parents' B&B guests. Matt has to doss down at his pal's place near the quay when he's here.'

Lucy made the coffee and carried the two mugs to the table. 'Biscuits in the tin,' she said. 'Help yourself.'

Penny took a chocolate-covered one and ate it with speed. 'I didn't have time to get any lunch.'

'Feel free to eat the lot then.'

She helped herself to more. 'You're too good to me.'

'You were going to fill me in about the rats.'

Penny pulled a face. 'You must have gathered that Matt's obsessive about them.'

'He likes rats?' Lucy was astonished.

'Getting rid of them. St Agnes and Gugh are clear of them right now, though no one can be quite be sure. It's not official yet, anyway. They breed like anything, you see.'

'You need a pied piper then, enticing them all away.'

Penny laughed. 'At least they wouldn't be able to swim back to St Agnes. It's the furthest inhabited island away from the others. At very low tides at certain times of the year, you can walk between some of the islands, but St Agnes and Gugh are way out on their own.'

Lucy thought about this. She tried to visualise the map of the islands she had been looking at back at the farm. She was still trying to get her head round armies of rats swimming, or paddling, back to islands that had become their homes and Matt being intent on stopping them.

'Don't look so worried,' Penny said with a laugh.

'So rats are overrunning everywhere? I haven't seen any.'

'You see the signs around sometimes. Droppings. We're asked to report every time we do.'

'It's that important?'

'They're the biggest threat to shear-waters and stormy petrels on land because they nest in burrows.'

'Birds?'

'You didn't think they'd attack humans, did you?'

Lucy hadn't thought of anything except that nobody seemed to like them. But they couldn't help being rats. They were living things too. She opened her mouth to say so but then thought better of it. She could see from Penny's expression that here was a serious issue she felt strongly about on her brother's behalf. She had said that Matt represented a wildlife organisation. Of course he cared about birds just as Angus, her boss back in Truro, cared for prehistoric sites, and her father cared for studying and preserving marine life. Mum, too, had once been reduced to tears at the idea of seal culling. Lucy felt she was missing something here, something important.

'The islands are home to breeding populations of ground-nesting birds,' Penny said. 'They think about twenty thousand of them, but numbers have been dropping. And that's why the rats have to be exterminated. They eat the eggs, you see.'

'They kill them?' Lucy was horrified. 'How?'

'Poison. That's what Matt's been involved in studying over on St Agnes. The poison's put inside tubes so that the rats go in and take it, and it doesn't hurt the wildlife.'

'But rats *are* wildlife.'

'Matt's working on getting a lot more people involved in seabird conservation. It's important, you see. Encouraging the islands to make the most of the natural environment helps boost local incomes. All good stuff.'

Lucy hardly listened. All she could think of was that the proceeds raised at the Farm Open Event were going to this wildlife project whose members considered it right to kill, and Matt played an important part in it.

4

Matt was pleased with the way the afternoon had gone. A great deal of interest had been shown in the Seabird Recovery stall and several donations had been made. He must remember to get even more leaflets printed in time for the barbecue next week or they'd be running short. He had intended to ask Penny to remind him about this, but his last sight of her dripping wet wouldn't have been a good moment.

Maybe she'd be back soon, and her new friend with her. His lips curved into a smile as he thought of Lucy's kindness. Penny could hardly have hung around in the condition she was in, and getting herself home on her bike straight away would have been decidedly unpleasant.

Inside the barn there was ample space on one of the trestle tables, as most of the farm produce on sale there had been purchased. The young stall-holder was looking very pleased with himself, as well he might. 'Is this the first time you've had your own stall, Carl?' Matt asked him.

The boy grinned. 'Not the last, either. All my young carrots went, and most of the bags of salad stuff. The visitors liked them. There's a chap staying next door who's keen on birds. Did you meet him? Sounded a bit of an expert.'

Matt hesitated. 'I don't think so.'

'Tall, in a khaki shirt. Very long shorts. Hiking boots.'

'You noticed a lot.'

'He kicked the leg of the table, that's why.'

'On purpose?'

'People were pushing. He bought a lot.'

'Can I lay out a few of my wares here, Carl, since you don't need the space now?'

'Feel free. I'm packing up anyway.

You can take the rest if you want. All fresh stuff. I dug up a lot of it up early this morning.'

Matt eyed the three bunches of spring onions and a couple of bags of salad leaves. 'I might just do that. Thanks.'

He placed the offerings on the ground near his box of spare leaflets. The crowds were thinning now. It was a vain hope that his stall would attract much more interest, but it gave him an excuse to stay a while longer. Penny's bike was still there, so she would be returning for it. There was always the hope that someone else would come back with her.

It was great for Josh Hammond that his cousin was able to drop everything and come to help him out at such short notice. Miranda had looked pale last Tuesday afternoon when he'd seen her on the crossing to the mainland. The woman with her seemed to get on well with her, carrying her bag for her up to the top deck and telling her to be careful as she tripped on the bottom step. Matt had mentioned to Josh that he had seen his wife on board the *Scillonian*, but hadn't gone into details. He wished now that he had filled him in a bit, even though Josh, strangely withdrawn, hadn't asked.

Here was Penny now, flushed and enthusiastic. 'About time too,' Matt said.

'Sorry. Were you waiting for me? I met someone.'

'There are plenty of them about.'

'Don't be like that, Matt.'

'So who is this someone?'

'He's here to study the nesting sites of storm petrels and shearwaters. Terns too. He's staying in Pear Tree next door at Polwhenna for the next couple of weeks. Says he's an enthusiast.'

'Does he, now. You soon found that out.'

'Lucy introduced us and we got talking. What's wrong with that?'

'Does Lucy like him?'

'Why wouldn't she? He's one of their clients.'

Matt balanced the spring onions and bags of salad leaves on top of his box of leaflets and heaved it up. 'It's a pity your chap isn't an archaeologist,' he said. 'You could really have got going on your favourite subject of the moment.'

Penny made a face at him. 'Makes a change from rats. Lucy would appreciate that.'

'You think so? You can help me carry some of these things to the car. I'll sling your bike on the roof rack.'

Penny smiled as she did what he'd asked, but her mind was plainly on other things. Matt had to admit that his was too, and they had a silent drive down to Pengarth House, their parents' place overlooking the wide channel between St Mary's and Tresco. The vacancies board had been taken down, he noticed, but he couldn't imagine that it would be for long. It was time he started looking for a suitable place on his own now that his job on the islands had been made permanent — a piece of luck he hadn't looked for. He had the rats to thank for that.

* * *

'Annie gone walkabout?'

Lucy looked round from pegging some towels on the washing line. Tanya's tone of voice this Monday morning was surprisingly cheerful. She was wearing a brightly striped T-shirt and looked in the bloom of health. Perhaps the Scilly air was agreeing with her. 'She's helping Josh cut back some of the ivy on the wall in the vegetable garden.'

'Helping Josh?'

'It's allowed.'

'Too right it is. But that garden's out of sight.'

'You're not suggesting . . . '

'I'll go and give them a hand.'

Lucy watched her go, deep in thought. Tanya continued to surprise her: one moment argumentative, the next charming. And now she was suspicious when there was nothing to be suspicious about. Before Tanya appeared at breakfast time, Josh had said that the ivy needed to be removed. 'Dusty work,' he said.

'I'll do it,' Annie had volunteered unexpectedly. 'I'm a right hand at weed disposal, even if ivy isn't a weed.'

Lucy was pleased to see that not only had Josh made a decision about something, but he was carrying it out immediately. His lethargy had made her anxious, and it was hard to know what to do about it without sounding too bossy. He had always been a laid-back sort of person, but since Miranda's disappearance his lack of interest in Polwhenna was disturbing.

There were some bills to settle, and Josh needed more supplies of hand-wash and the green bathroom cleaner to be ordered online. First, though, Lucy would get the booking page of the website up to date after she had dealt with any fresh enquiries that had come by post as well as by email.

Some necessary purchases at the post office needed to be done in the afternoon, and Josh suggested that Lucy take the car down into Hugh Town to see to it.

'Good idea. Is there anything else I can do for you while I'm there?'

Josh took a bite of the huge sandwich he had made for himself. 'The butcher's?' he said when he had swallowed it. 'Call in and make yourself known, why don't you? Check what supplies of meat we have and place an order. He'll deliver. Then feel free to look round the place.'

They were sitting out in the sunshine to eat their lunch. Lucy looked up and smiled as Annie came to join them, her plate piled high with rolls and cheese. She set down the glass of apple juice she was carrying, put her plate down too, and sat down.

'Hungry?' Josh said, raising his eyebrows.

She giggled. 'Aren't I always?'

'It's after all that hard work,' Lucy said. 'Where's Tanya?'

Annie looked awkward. 'In the shower, I think.'

'Lucy's taking the car down to town later, if you fancy a trip down too,' Josh said.

'No worries,' Annie replied. 'The beach for us this afternoon. All that lovely sand. A swim too, with luck.'

Josh looked doubtful. 'The sea's still cold. And it's rocky on the waterline.'

'Right. Sunbathing instead then. That'll do me.'

Lucy thought of the beautiful pool here at Polwhenna and wondered if all the occupants of the cottages had gone out for the day.

Annie looked up as Tanya, her hair wet, joined them and flopped down beside Josh. 'Aren't you eating anything?' he said.

'Too exhausted.'

'All right?' said Annie. 'You didn't . . . ?'

Tanya beamed at her.

'Ace!'

Lucy finished her own meal and got up. It seemed that the girls would be occupied for the afternoon and she was free to be on her own for an hour or two, which was good. Josh had already given her a street map of the town in case she had forgotten the layout, and suggested a good place for parking. All she had to do was wash her plate, tumbler and utensils and get ready to go.

★   ★   ★

Lucy was surprised there hadn't been more changes since her last visit to the island. A few new buildings, that was all. There was still the special atmosphere about the place that made it seem a world apart. The smell of salt lingered in the air too, and between the buildings the sea glinted blue in the sunshine. Everywhere there was the cry of gulls.

She wandered down to the quay,

where people were waiting to board the small boats to take them to the island of their choice for the afternoon. She wished she was going off somewhere too. Maybe she would on another free afternoon. Where would she choose? St Martin's, Bryer, Tresco, St Agnes? Then she saw a board advertising an archaeological walk on one of the uninhabited islands. How Angus would love that! She sat down on a bench for a few moments to watch people board the various boats and to think of the elderly man who had been so kind to her in the months since her break-up with Tom.

Angus had talked sometimes of retirement, but it had come to nothing. He had never married and had no close family, so there was no one to urge him to make the sensible decision to sell up and start a new life elsewhere. Lucy had often reminded him of his interest in prehistory, and pointed out that he would be free to travel and visit some of the ancient sites he had been reading about, and perhaps get to know like-minded people. But after an initial interest in the idea, he had done nothing.

So sad, Lucy thought as she watched two families of teenage children and their parents board the boat for Samson. The next moment Penny came rushing up, her ponytail of auburn hair bobbing. She caught sight of Lucy and stopped.

'Hi there, Lucy. I'm off to Samson on the archaeological walk. Why don't you come too?'

'Wish I could. Things to do. Don't miss the boat!'

The boats were filling up fast. Moments later, the first one edged away from the quay and headed out across the water. When at last they were all away, Lucy got up and set off on another wander through the narrow streets, intending to do a bit of exploring on the other side of the narrow strip of land on which the small town had grown up.

She came to a newish building that

was the tourist office, and better still, another beautiful beach of silver sand with the sea shining turquoise and clear in the afternoon sunshine. She had known the beach was here, but its sheer beauty took her by surprise, and she stood and gazed for several moments. Here she would stay for a while, with a handful of useful leaflets from the tourist office and anything else informative that she could study at her leisure.

Some of the leaflets on the stand were familiar because she had seen them in the folder Josh had left by the computer for her to look at. She picked up one or two others at random, then saw that on the counter was some more information printed on sheets of A4 paper.

'They've just been brought in, m'dear,' the middle-aged woman behind the counter told her. 'The annual barbecue at Pengarth is always popular. Donations for that one on the night.'

Lucy smiled her thanks for the information. She liked what she saw of the soft grey hair tied back from a cheerful face by a band of green ribbon that exactly matched the woman's blouse. Lucy saw from the badge she was wearing that she was Miss Marcia Fletcher. Marcia was a pretty name and suited the owner well.

'Oh, and there's the latest timetable for the community bus. You'll want that.'

Before Lucy could answer, some more people came in to check the poster advertising the craft fair in the town hall in two weeks' time. Two of them, with their heads together, made a show of examining the leaflet stand. Lucy, conscious of their murmured voices, tried not to listen; but the fact that they were almost whispering drew more attention than if they had raised their voices to communicate with each other.

'Such a shame,' the first one muttered. 'But I saw it coming. Didn't you, Peggy?'

'Me too. Poor chap. He'll be lost now without her.'

'I heard she'd gone off with a visitor, not caring who saw them. Didn't even have the decency to leave a note.'

'Considered herself a cut above the rest of us and could do what she liked.'

'I never liked her.'

'Have you seen him since?'

The reply in hushed tones was lost to Lucy as the door opened again and others came in. Among them she saw Matt Henderson with a sheaf of papers in his hand. He gave her a brief smile as he went to the counter.

'These are for you, Marcia,' he said. 'The next seabird cruise. Give it a bit of publicity, will you?'

'Don't I always, young man?'

'Always, for us all, dear Marcia.'

'Get away with you. Have you no work to do?'

'As much as ever.'

Still stunned by what she had overheard, Lucy was hardly aware of Matt's hand on her elbow steering her through the open doorway.

'Something bothering you?' he said.

'You look as if you've seen a ghost.'

'They were talking about my cousin, I'm sure they were. Those women near the leaflet stand. All lies. I didn't know what to do.'

Matt laughed. 'Gossips, the pair of them.'

'The things they were saying . . . '

'Did they mention names?'

'No, but — '

'Not worth bothering about then.'

'But they were talking about Josh.'

'There's a place along here. Coffee, I think, good and strong.'

She pulled away from him. 'Didn't you hear me?'

'I heard you good and strong. Like the coffee. Listen to me, Lucy. Everyone knows what those two are like. No one takes any notice of them, and you shouldn't either. Have some sense.'

To Lucy's dismay, tears welled up in her throat. She swallowed hard, unable to understand why he seemed to be attacking her for her actions, or lack of them, when she was too weak to confront those women. His calmness was infuriating. A shot of anger filled her.

'I have my own thoughts and beliefs,' she said. 'My own feelings too, especially about the wildlife you insist on killing for no good reason.'

'You shouldn't make quick judgements based on nothing more than hearsay, Lucy. Come on the next seabird cruise, why don't you?'

'Why should I do that?'

'You'll see nesting sites on the islands we pass. You'll learn how important our work is.' A flicker of sadness seemed to touch him, and then was gone.

'What sort of boat do you use?' she said. 'One of those big ones?'

'A family boat. Just a smallish one with an outboard engine. We take about five or six interested people at a time. Mum's twin brother owned the boat and it came to me when he died. I was named after him.'

He seemed about to say more, but let a silence form between them instead.

Lucy cleared her throat, surprised he didn't insist that she book in at once.

'I was out of order just now,' she said at last. 'But I know how important Josh's work is. He's just trying to exist without someone who means the world to him.'

'A lot of people do that,' said Matt.

5

Lucy's anger had melted as quickly as it had arisen, and her legs felt as if they would give way at any moment. She didn't usually react so quickly, and in such a childish way, so what had come over her? Josh and Miranda were well-known on the island. People would be bound to talk. She must get used to it and do all she could to support Josh instead of lashing out at Matt. What had she been thinking of? Ashamed, she looked away from him and saw that the beach was still as silvery beautiful as it had been before, and the sea as sparkling in the glare of the sun. Somehow, though, its beauty seemed dimmed so that she could no longer feel it.

'I think I'd like that coffee, please,' she said, her voice low.

He nodded. 'This way then.'

He chose a table outside, and they sat in the shade of a canopy that cast pink shadows over them. Neither spoke as they waited for their drinks to cool a little. The silence was restful, and Lucy began to feel calmness stealing over her. She moved a little in her seat and Matt cast a questioning glance at her. She smiled.

Other people came to fill some of the other tables, and on the beach a few families settled, enjoying the surroundings that once more to Lucy seemed alive again because she was feeling so much better.

'All right now?' Matt said, smiling too. He raised his cup to his lips, drank and put it down again. 'Or am I being too insensitive?'

'No, no, not that.' She was still worried about Josh, but she couldn't mention it. Enough had been said about her cousin behind his back as it was. He needed time to come to terms with what was happening in his marriage and what the future held for him here on Scilly if Miranda didn't return.

'I saw Penny a little while ago,' she said in an attempt at normal conversation. 'She was getting on of the boats down on the quay, the one to Samson.'

'It's the first walk of that sort this season,' Matt said. 'Penny's free to do this now she's finished school after her A-levels.'

'She's only eighteen?'

'Eighteen going on twenty-five. Mum and Dad have given her the afternoon off. She's working for them at the guesthouse for a year before she makes up her mind what she wants to do.'

'A gap year?'

'A gap year without moving off anywhere else like a lot of her friends plan to do. She likes to be different, you see.'

Lucy laughed. 'She's a great girl.'

Matt looked pleased. 'Not everyone thinks so.'

'They don't?'

'Dad, for one. He'd have liked a little

71

princess for a daughter, I think. Instead he's got a hoyden, as he calls her.'

'A hoyden?' Lucy thought of the lively girl who looked good even in the rough clothes she wore to drive the tractor. She had leapt nimbly up into the vehicle, elegantly even, and Lucy found it hard to believe she was a schoolgirl.

Matt picked up his empty cup, examined it closely and then put it down again. 'The trouble is, she isn't really sure what she wants to do, and that worries Mum a bit. At the moment Penny thinks she'd like to run her own adventure park, somewhere where there are towering cliffs to climb and abseil down. Meanwhile, she's earning her keep as a skivvy at Pengarth.'

'Like I'm doing at Polwhenna.'

'A little different, I think.'

'Maybe.'

'How's it going?'

'Pretty well. I'm only just settling in.'

'Have you done this sort of thing before?'

'My job is helping the owner of a bookshop.' Lucy's face clouded.

'You're missing him?' Matt said quietly.

'Angus? I'm sad for him. The business is running down, and I don't know what he'll do without it. He's holding on to the bitter end, and I'm afraid he'll lose out financially. He's too old to change now.'

The expression on Matt's face lightened. 'Too old?'

'Well into his seventies. He's like a kind grandfather to me. I hate to see him so despondent. He's given me as much time as I need to help out here, but I'm thinking of handing in my notice so he doesn't feel obliged to pay me anymore. I'm afraid he'll be rather hurt, but I need to do it.'

'Being cruel to be kind?'

'Something like that.' She thought suddenly of Tom breaking their commitment to each other so swiftly. For the first time she felt a tinge of understanding, and of gratitude too.

This was an uplifting thought that seemed to free something in her she hadn't known was there. She smiled at Matt. 'Anyway, I love it at Polwhenna.'

'Scilly's a great place to be,' Matt said. 'I'm lucky that my work means spending a lot of time over here.'

Lucy didn't want to think about what his work entailed. Just for a moment, as they sat here in the sunshine, she had pushed that to the back of her mind. She felt his glance on her and felt a little awkward that she had accepted his hospitality and yet had only condemnation for what she knew meant a great deal to him.

Matt drained the last of his coffee. 'So, d'you fancy — '

'The seabird cruise?'

'I wasn't thinking of suggesting that if you're not interested. How about our barbecue next Saturday?'

'The one the tourist board are advertising?'

'That's the one.'

'In aid of your work?'

'You don't have to contribute anything if you don't want to, Lucy. Penny would like you to come, and she's helping to organise it. We have barbecues on the beach in front of Pengarth quite often, weather permitting. A lovely spot with the sun going down. Will you come?'

'I'll think about it.'

He smiled again and stood up. 'Duty calls now, I'm afraid. I must be on my way. I'm pleased we met.'

'Me too.' For a moment she hesitated, wanting to say something more, but not quite knowing what.

At her car she paused and looked at her watch. Just for a change, she could follow the road round the other way to Polwhenna through Old Town to see a different part of the island.

The trees shading the narrow road were a surprise because she couldn't remember them from childhood visits. Meeting the community bus doing its round trip was another surprise, but it shouldn't have been. Carefully she reversed the required distance and then waited for the bus to pass. As she did so, she caught sight of Tanya and Annie sitting on the back seat with someone else she recognised, the young man staying in one of their properties. He had come alone to Polwhenna to give himself the time and space he needed to settle down to some serious writing. Ornithology was his subject, he had told her.

The telephone was ringing as Lucy went into the house, but stopped as she was about to pick up the receiver. 'Number withheld', she was told by the disembodied voice when she checked. Miranda?

She didn't know why she should think it was her, except that no one else was likely to withhold a number. The door was unlocked, so Josh must be somewhere about, and she set off to find him, looking first in the house and then outside. At last she gave up, made herself a coffee and carried it out to their private patio.

Josh came twenty minutes later, rubbing his eyes and looking surprised to see her.

'You didn't hear the phone?' she said.

The wooden bench appeared to be lower than he had anticipated and he sat down on it with a thump. He looked at her, a vague expression on his face. 'I've been taking things easy.' He yawned. 'Did it matter?'

She got up. 'I'll make you a coffee. Don't move.' Not that he looked at all likely to do so, but she watched him through the kitchen window while the kettle boiled to make sure. He was certainly in a strange mood.

'The phone number was withheld,' she said, placed his mug down in front of him and sitting down. 'I wondered if you had any idea who it could be.'

Josh shook his head. 'None at all.'

'I thought maybe it could be Miranda.'

'Miranda?' Suddenly he looked up and smiled. 'D'you think it could?'

Lucy almost suggested he should

phone her to check but then changed her mind. This was something he must decide for himself.

'She might ring back,' he said.

* * *

Josh changed from his usual drab working clothes into clean shorts and a colourful shirt for the barbecue on Saturday. The red and orange stripes were startling to say the least, but Lucy approved when he came downstairs and waited for the girls to appear. It was good to see that he had thrown off his lethargy for this evening at least.

'All set then, Josh?' she said. 'Aren't Tanya and Annie coming down in the car with us?'

'Didn't you see them? They've already gone.'

'Keen to get there, obviously. Especially with Simon Hartley.'

'Who?'

'Wake up, Josh. Our tenant in Pear Tree.'

'I don't think that's such a good idea.'

'So what d'you think is going to happen? One of them going off with Simon Hartley to the mainland without a backward glance?' Lucy clamped a hand over her mouth in dismay. What sort of fool was she to come out with that?

Josh seemed hardly to have heard. He picked up his car keys from the hall table and looked at them, deep in thought. 'We're off to the same place after all,' he conceded. 'Miranda always said I worried too much over things that were never going to happen.'

The wrong things, Lucy thought. He didn't appear to worry about Miranda or her well-being.

They journeyed down the road towards Hugh Town in silence. Pengarth House was in a beautiful position overlooking Tresco and two of the other islands, Bryer and Samson. This evening the sea was like silver, with hardly a ripple, and the air felt balmy. The scent of honeysuckle wafted across to them, and there was the distant cry of some seabird Lucy didn't recognise.

Josh parked a short distance away. Others were arriving too, some by car and others on foot. Lucy recognised Marcia Fletcher from the tourist office and smiled at her. She looked different this evening, in a long skirt of floaty material and a sleeveless blouse that made her look younger than Lucy remembered.

'Hello, my dear,' Marcia greeted her. 'I'm glad you could come. And Josh too. My, don't you look the part.'

'Ah, Marcia. It's good to see you,' Josh said.

'I wouldn't miss it for the world. And neither would Danny. He's here somewhere. He's got something he wants to tell you.'

They followed a crowd of people onto the beach opposite the house. This was a square double-fronted building that stood in its own small garden, which was bounded by a low stone wall. The front door was wide open, with people going in and out carrying trays of covered food they placed on long trestle tables someone had set up near the flat grassy area that bordered the sandy beach.

Lucy couldn't see Tanya or Annie, but the large figure of Simon Hartley towered above others near the water's edge, so they must be around some- where. He caught sight of her and waved.

It was a cheerful scene this early evening in June, and Lucy found herself wondering where Matt was. There were two barbecues set up. Someone had lit a driftwood fire over by the rocks, and the smoke from that floated pleasantly across and mingled with the smell of cooking beef burgers and sausages. She saw the farmer's son, Carl Birkett, feeding the flames with a fresh stack of wood someone had brought him.

At that moment Penny appeared, calling out to a group near the fire and ordering them to help her carry out the plates and cutlery. They all, laughing and joking, followed her into the house. Lucy went in too, wondering if Penny would notice her in the bustling crowd.

'Matt's looking for you,' someone told her when everyone in front of her had picked up their load and staggered out with it. The woman who spoke had short spiky hair, and Lucy recognised her as one of the two gossipers she had met in the tourist office.

'Oh, right. Thanks,' Lucy said. What was this place like, for goodness sake? Could she do nothing without everyone knowing who she was and why she was here? But on the other hand, wasn't that what she wanted — to feel she belonged?

'So where is he?' she said.

'Right here,' said a familiar voice. 'There's nothing for you to do here, Lucy. Penny can cope. Let's get outside.'

Across the water, dusk was beginning to blur the outlines of the islands. There were lights out here now, dotted about among the rocks bordering the beach, giving a magical feel to the scene. Lucy smiled to see the reflections on the wet sand where the tide was going out.

'Fancy something to eat?' Matt asked her.

There were jacket potatoes and pork chops slightly burnt at the edges. Lucy took one of each, and some crispy bacon. More lights illuminated the table laden with a variety of salads and a magnificent cheese board. Lucy saw Annie pile her plate high, and Tanya too, in skimpy shorts and a scarlet top.

Matt led the way to a quieter spot where the grass met the sand.

'This is a lovely thing to do,' Lucy said as she settled herself on a grassy overhang that made a good seat. 'I'm fine here, Matt, if you need to mingle.'

'You want to get rid of me?'

'Perhaps not until we've eaten our meal.'

His eyes twinkled at her in the light from a nearby lamp. 'There's plenty more to eat, I can tell you. And desserts yet, you know. Penny's proud of the selection she's got together.'

'What about your mum and dad?'

'Last seen talking to your cousin. They went off with Josh into the house, I think, so it must be something serious. You'll have to meet them another day.'

The noise level was increasing now and conversation was difficult. They went up twice more to replenish their plates, and Matt found drinks for them, which he carried carefully back on a small tray. 'Mum's dandelion and burdock,' he said. 'Or how about some lemon and ginger? I've brought both.'

Penny joined them, bringing with her some of Matt's colleagues carrying cans of something that must have been a lot stronger, judging by the cheerful noise they were making.

'They always get like this,' Penny told her. 'Take no notice, Lucy. Non-alcoholic is the rule for tonight. It's tradition. But you wouldn't think so, would you?'

'Where have all this crowd come from?' Lucy asked.

Penny grinned. 'Who cares? There's loads of food.'

'It's never been like this before,' Matt said. 'A far noisier proposition than usual. Totally unexpected.'

'It's great, Matt,' Penny said. 'You'll be raking in the money. Your birds'll be laughing their heads off in their nesting burrows. Don't you think so, Lucy?'

Lucy smiled but didn't reply. This was the first indication that it wasn't merely a social occasion, and she didn't want to be reminded of that. Later someone produced an accordion and some dancing started up. She hoped that every self-respecting bird on the islands had the sense to keep well clear.

Just as Josh seemed to be doing after the serious talk with Matt's parents.

6

Josh hunched himself over the steering wheel on the homeward journey. He seemed too absorbed in his thoughts to think of making conversation, so Lucy kept quiet. She had a lot to think about too, mainly about the new people she had met and chatted to. They were a friendly crowd, but she was sure she would never be able to remember all their names. The first few were easy, but then she had given up and decided to relax and enjoy herself.

Josh had only joined them on the beach at the very end, when a few people had already gone and others were making signs that they should be on their way too. Matt had already offered to run Lucy home when she was ready to go.

'No?' he'd said with eyebrows raised. 'Josh drove me down. I'd better wait for him or he'll think I've got myself drowned or something.'

Matt had laughed but he seemed disappointed. To her surprise, Lucy was too. He was good company when he wasn't talking about his work, although to be fair he hadn't tried to convince her of anything since she had made her opinions clear.

Back at Polwhenna, Josh drew up at the side of the house and sat for a moment staring straight ahead.

'Josh,' Lucy said, 'is anything wrong?'

At that moment there was a roar as another car came sweeping in. It pulled up alongside and Tanya and Annie piled out, laughing. Simon Hartley emerged slowly and stretched both arms above his head. It was plain to see that all three had had a good time. Simon gazed proudly down at his two passengers. 'All right, ladies?'

'Ace,' Tanya laughed.

Lucy and Josh got out of their car too and closed the doors. 'Your lights are on,' Josh said to Simon. Annie giggled.

In an exaggerated way, Simon got back into his vehicle and switched them off.

'I think we could all do with a hot drink,' Lucy said.

'Not me,' said Simon. 'I'm for bed.' He lumbered off, yawning. The others sat round the table in the kitchen while Tanya plugged in the kettle and made tea. She put an extra spoonful of sugar in Josh's mug and handed it to him in silence. Both she and Annie talked in subdued voices until he had drunk it, scalding hot, and then Tanya got up to pour him another.

This was a side of Tanya that Lucy hadn't seen, and she marvelled at how sensitively the girl was treating him. So had she got Tanya wrong? It certainly seemed like it. But then she remembered one other occasion when Tanya had seemed to sympathise with Annie over something for all of five minutes, only to show disinterest a short time afterward with a hurtful remark.

From what they were saying, Lucy

gathered that the evening had been a success. The girls had got together with a group of young people who made a point of meeting up on a Wednesday evening down in Hugh Town. Sometimes there were musical events on one of the off islands, and they never missed those.

Lucy had joined up with Penny towards the end of the evening, and that was good too. They had talked about Lucy's job over on the mainland, which already seemed to be part of a former life that was fast becoming insignificant. She hadn't thought of Tom all evening — or for the last day or two, if she were honest. Her concern for the elderly Angus Pellow was still there, though.

'So your boss likes all things archaeological,' said Penny. 'Plenty of that sort of stuff over here on the islands. We've got the most remains of burial chambers and the like per mile than any other place in the UK. Did you know that? I'll show you some of them if you like. There are some good walks.'

'Yes, I'd like that,' Lucy had said, amused at her young friend's proprietorial manner.

So it looked as if three of them from Polwhenna were happy with the evening. Only Josh, sunk in gloom, was not.

★　★　★

Sudden bursts of heavy rain the next morning made any thought of walking anywhere impossible. Even Penny, with her total disregard for the elements, would surely think better of getting in touch, as she had said she might. In any case, Lucy was worried about Josh. She wished he would tell her what was troubling him, but she dare not ask. His manner had shown only too clearly that he wouldn't welcome any questioning.

In a short lull between showers after breakfast, Lucy made a point of visiting the new people in Tamarisk to check that all was well. The door onto the patio in front of their cottage was closed, and there was no answer to her knock. Maybe they had made an early start today, hopefully before the first squall had come sweeping across. She had welcomed the Cooks late the previous afternoon, and Rick Cook had handed her a card.

'Keep that safe,' he said. 'My mobile number. It might come in handy.' She had pocketed it and thanked him.

Now she turned away and ran for the house before the rain started again. Annie was in the kitchen, washing up. Lucy picked a tea towel off the rack.

'Resting,' Annie told her when Lucy asked where Tanya was.

'You had a late night.'

'We all did.'

'That's true. Josh anywhere about?'

Annie shrugged. She looked pale, Lucy noticed, and there was no sign of a smile on her face.

'You're okay, Annie?'

'This rain's horrible.'

'It won't last. It'll clear up suddenly, you'll see.'

Annie looked unconvinced. She placed the last plate in the drainer and emptied the water.

This looked like a case of homesickness, Lucy thought. She wished she could think of something absorbing for Annie to do that would keep her mind occupied. Or something physical. 'A swim in the pool?' she suggested.

'Won't Josh mind?'

'Not in this weather. No one else will want it. I'll take the responsibility.' Somehow she didn't think that Josh would care what they did. He had more important things on his mind at the moment.

'I'll be wet anyway.'

'Come on then, let's do it.'

'You too?'

'Your partner in crime.'

Annie giggled.

Five minutes later they plunged in. After the initial shock, Lucy began to enjoy herself. Annie streamed ahead, slicing through the water like a seal. Even a heavy deluge of rain didn't stop her, though Lucy doubted whether she had ever done anything like this before. She herself hadn't either, come to think of it, so it was probably a new experience for both of them.

At last they had had enough and climbed out, shivering. 'Back to the house for hot showers,' said Lucy. She pulled out her towel from beneath the sunbed she had chosen to keep it dry. 'First to be finished get the kettle on.'

The rain had stopped now and the struggling sun was doing its best to make an appearance. Annie's cheeks glowed pink. Things were looking up.

★   ★   ★

Lucy spent the morning checking the computer for more booking enquiries and found three. She replied at once and then spent time making sure the website was up to date. By lunchtime it seemed that her weather predictions were correct, and shortly afterwards Penny appeared wearing old jeans and a tatty anorak that had definitely seen better days.

'Are you still on?' she said when Lucy opened the back door to her and she stepped inside.

'Definitely.'

'I've left my bike round the side. Not many people about.'

'All off somewhere or other, I expect.'

'I hope we will be soon, but not with you wearing those clothes.'

Lucy looked down at her navy and turquoise top and brand-new jeans. 'That's because it's Sunday,' she said.

'The ground's just as rough going as on any other day. Boggy too, in places. You'd better get changed.

'Where are we heading?'

'The coastal path round from Shearwater Cove to Bant's Carn.'

'Sounds good.'

They set off down the rutted track to the beach and by the time they got there the sky was clear of even a wisp of cloud. Out at sea the Eastern Isles looked bright. The path that Penny took narrowed between the growing bracken that darkened the legs of their jeans with raindrops. The bright flowers of red campion intermingled with it, and there were a few tall pink foxgloves too, sticking up above everything else. Penny went at such a speed that Lucy was breathless by the time they reached the top of the rising ground.

'The view's worth it anyway,' she said.

Penny turned and grinned at her.

'Too fast for you?'

Lucy wasn't going to admit it. 'Not now it's downhill again,' she said.

The winding path widened as it levelled, and Penny slowed her pace a little as they went round the next bend.

'We'll come to Bant's Carn soon,' she said. 'It's an entrance tomb, the best-preserved one on Scilly. We'll pass some others on the way, but that's the best. There's the remains of an Iron Age village too a bit further on. They think it was lived in for about five hundred years up until the Romans left. But Bant's Carn is much older. Bronze Age.'

'So how long ago was the Bronze Age?'

'From about 4,000 years ago until about 3,000, I think. Something like that anyway. It's near enough.'

Lucy was impressed. 'How do you know all that?'

'Remembered it from my schooldays.'

'That makes you sound elderly.'

Penny laughed. 'I feel I am sometimes.' She held back a bramble straddling the path. Further on she paused again. 'There were a lot of people living here permanently from around 2,500 B.C. The sea level was much lower then, so Scilly would have been a single mass of land, would you believe?'

Lucy gazed out across the water. 'It's hard to imagine. So when did it change?'

Penny wrinkled her nose. 'It happened gradually, of course. But probably the islands were much the same as they are today by the end of the Roman period.'

They moved on, and at last they reached a large open space now dotted with variously shaped granite rocks among the turf. On a crest ahead of them was the entrance grave they had come to see.

Lucy had expected a gloomier place with an atmosphere of sadness. To her surprise there were sparkles of sunlight on the four huge granite slabs that formed the roof of the burial chamber, and daisies decorating the grass. Beyond was the cobalt-blue of the sea, the paler sky, Tresco's low-lying shore, and the twin humps of the island she knew was Samson. 'Can we go inside?' she said.

'Why not?

Lucy bent her head as she went in past the clumps of bracken that decorated each side of the entrance.

Shafts of sunlight trickled through a few gaps in the walls, and there was gravel underfoot. In the niches, small round-leaved plants poked their heads. At the end she turned round, and at that moment her mobile phone rang. She pulled it out of her pocket.

'Oh no!'

'Good timing,' Penny said from outside.

7

Josh knew that Lucy and Penny had gone walking and by now could be some way away from Polwhenna. Making friends was good for Lucy, and he had been pleased when she had told him of her plans. He could have wished it had been anyone less scatty than Penny, though, and more her own age. He had already tripped over that ancient bike she had left propped up at the side of the house, in a prime position for anyone wandering round that way to do themselves an injury.

He was thinking of the consequences of that when Annie found him in the vegetable garden, having just made a start on hoeing between the rows of lettuces.

'Josh?' She looked distressed.

'Annie.'

'You'd better come, Josh. There's

something wrong at Tamarisk. It looks as if the front door's been blown open. It's just hanging there looking odd. It's been tight shut until now.'

'And there's no one there?'

'I knocked and called out.'

He went with her to investigate. It was in his mind to ask her why she hadn't shut the door, but he could see from her expression that she wanted him to see for himself.

He looked inside. 'Anyone at home?'

Of course there wasn't. The empty atmosphere told him that at once, and everything was far too tidy. He kicked off his boots, and Annie followed him in and exclaimed at the lack of personal belongings anyone would expect to find when a place was occupied. There was nothing here that didn't belong to the property.

'We'll check the bedrooms,' Josh said, tight-lipped.

Empty coat hangers rattled as he pulled open the wardrobe door in the double room. The drawers in the chest by the window had nothing in them, and neither had the bedside lockers.

Annie had found nothing of a personal nature in the other bedroom either. 'Done a bunk?' she said, wide-eyed.

'Looks like it.'

'So what do we do?'

'Their mobile phone number will be on the computer. I'll try to contact them. Nothing for you to do, Annie. Thanks for having the sense to come and find me. Where's Tanya?'

'She's gone to meet Andy. He was at the barbie last night.'

'And left you on your own?'

She looked at him as if he didn't know what he was talking about. And perhaps he didn't, he thought. He was devoid of common sense, and humour too. Miranda had told him that often enough. But common sense told him now that it was unlikely these people had left the island, and it would be a good thing to try to contact them.

He got through at once. A surprisingly cheerful voice answered but refused to say where he was or why he and his wife had left. How could he tell if this was a genuine call?

'Of course it's genuine,' Josh said, his voice terse. 'I'm speaking from Polwhenna, and I'd like an answer. Is that clear?'

'And I'll make it clear that we want our money back. The place was disgusting. We dealt with a young lady previously. I'll speak only to her.' And he clicked off.

★ ★ ★

'They're mad,' Penny said.

'Or devious.' Lucy thought they would take ages returning to Polwhenna by the winding coastal path, but Penny pointed out that it was far quicker by road. And so it proved.

'And Josh just said there were complaints about the property and they wanted a refund?' Penny said as they set out.

'That's about it.'

Penny's indignant expression was almost laughable. 'That's ridiculous. What complaints could they possibly have?'

'That's the question.'

'And Josh is taking this seriously?'

'It *is* serious, Penny. Think about it. This could damage our reputation even if they haven't any grounds for their complaint, and I'm certain they haven't. I always check each property before the new people go in.'

'And you did this time?'

'Of course.'

'So what will Josh do then?'

'He wants me to phone Mr Cook on the landline from Polwhenna so he doesn't get my mobile number. There's just a chance that I can cool things, as he insisted on speaking to me.'

'That's sensible.'

After that Penny was silent, and Lucy said no more. They were walking as swiftly as they could and she needed all her breath for the effort of keeping up. Josh had sounded depressed, and no wonder. His voice had lightened immediately at hearing that Lucy would return at once to deal with the issue. She hoped his faith in her was justified.

He was waiting by the front gate. 'We've come back to put up a fight,' Penny called out to him. 'Lead on, Josh. I want to see what all the fuss is about.'

Lucy checked that the loudspeaker was on and then dialled the mobile number from the card Rick Cook had given her. 'This is Lucy from Polwhenna, Mr Cook. I understand you have a problem with your accommodation here?'

'I'll say. The condition of the place is appalling. My wife refused to stay a moment longer. In fact she was hysterical when we found the dead flies in every drawer and the dead rat under the sink.'

'What?'

'Disgusting. Some poison must have been stored there for killing rats. We've been hearing about that sort of thing.'

Penny gave a strangled laugh. 'The very idea!'

Lucy took a deep breath. 'I accompanied you into Tamarisk to show you round when you and Mrs Cook arrived late yesterday afternoon, if you remember,' she said. 'There was no mention then that the place wasn't up to standard.'

'You didn't show us under the sink or inside the drawers, did you?' His voice was triumphant.

'Everything was checked thoroughly before you arrived.'

'So you're calling me a liar?'

'I repeat that the property was seen to be of the highest standard in cleanliness, Mr Cook. I can say nothing more than that.'

'We want our money back and we'll see we get it.'

'That's not possible.'

'Then the tourist board will hear of this first thing tomorrow. The health and safety people too.'

Lucy did her best to keep calm.

'Then there's nothing more to be said.'

'Unless you see sense, of course. Otherwise I'll get online as well, and post the worst review you've ever seen.'

Lucy replaced the receiver and looked at Josh. 'Now what?'

He shrugged. 'We've had nothing like this happen before.'

'But he won't win, will he?'

'Let's take another a look inside the place,' Josh said.

Annie was sitting at the picnic table on the patio in front of Tamarisk. Behind her the door was now shut. She sprang up and propped it open. 'It was my turn to clean this one yesterday,' she said in a small voice.

'And you did it brilliantly,' Lucy assured her. 'I can vouch for that. No one's blaming you, Annie. It's all a pack of lies.'

'But who else can vouch for it?' Penny said. 'There's me, of course, but that won't be any good. We could be in this together.'

They were soon able to verify that no

dead rat skulked beneath the sink and no dead flies littered any of the drawers. 'Mr and Mrs Crook,' Penny said in heartfelt tones. Then she brightened. 'I know! Marcia Fletcher.'

Lucy felt a flicker of hope. 'From the tourist office?'

'Off duty of course, as it's Sunday, but she'd be perfect. It would be like an official inspection, wouldn't it? She'll come at once, I know she will. Dad's got her home number at Pengarth. The quicker the better. I'll phone him, shall I?'

Moments later, Josh, still looking slightly dazed, made the call to Marcia on his mobile and told her that Matt Henderson would be picking her up and bringing her to Polwhenna. Their gratitude to her for being willing to come was immense. 'Fifteen minutes,' he said to the others as he clicked off.

Marcia was all smiles as Matt ushered her round the side of the house to where the others were sitting outside Tamarisk. They all sprang up. Lucy knew that Matt would be with Marcia, but she felt a huge jolt of relief at seeing him.

He smiled at her, raising one eyebrow as if to display his confidence that all would be well. She smiled too, and felt the tension begin to slip away.

Marcia was wearing pink trousers and a cream cardigan buttoned to the neck. 'Now what's all this, then?' she said. 'Polwhenna falling down heavily on the cleanliness issue? I simply don't believe it.'

Lucy smiled. 'That's good to hear.'

Marcia took a notepad and a camera from her voluminous bag, then rustled about for a pen. 'I know I've got one somewhere. Ah, here it is. Now, Matt and I will do the checking. You come with us too, Josh. I see you've sense enough not to take this too seriously.'

'Oh, but we are,' Penny objected.

Marcia's smile was reassuring, and Matt gave Lucy a nod before he followed Marcia inside the building. 'They won't get away with it, you know,' he murmured.

It seemed that they wouldn't with the redoubtable Marcia on their side, but Lucy was glad to hear him say it.

⋆　⋆　⋆

The events of the afternoon had been decidedly unexpected. After the evening meal, and with the washing-up done, Lucy was glad to have a little time on her own to come to terms with it all. All signs of the earlier rain had vanished and the track down to the cove was completely dry. The evening had that pearly glow about it that she loved, and the scent from the honeysuckle where the track narrowed to a path seemed especially pungent in the soft air.

Instead of continuing to the beach, she veered off to the right and followed another more grassy path as it wound round some higher ground. She came to a stone stile and climbed nimbly over it, then paused to look back the way she had come. The tide was well out, and from here the expanse of sand looked almost white, decorated by a broken line of brown seaweed. Edging it were grey stones and boulders of all shapes and sizes, and beyond that the bright cerulean of the sea was streaked with paler shades of blue. Nearer at hand, the red campion and sorrel were doing their best to make their presence felt through the brambles and young bracken.

She walked on until she reached the end of the low grassy headland with its three dark trees on the skyline. Here she found a useful rocky outcrop for a seat. But even surrounded by all this beauty, the events of the afternoon were still with her. She felt again her sense of disbelief that anyone could act in such a despicable way. At the time it had seemed to her that it was somehow her fault and that she had been found wanting. Having Matt there made it seem almost worse. He had just arrived at his parents' place when Penny phoned for Marcia's telephone number and he took the call. He hadn't hesitated in arranging to bring Marcia up to Polwhenna himself with as much speed as possible.

To the three of them waiting outside while the inspection took place, the minutes had ticked slowly by. Lucy had tried to reassure Annie, who looked as pale as she had earlier in the day. At last the three others emerged, Marcia carrying her clipboard as if it was her prize possession, Josh looking grave, and Matt as calm as he always seemed but with a steely look to his jaw.

'Nothing at all to worry about,' he told them.

Josh frowned. 'Except for the bad publicity this will generate.'

'I'll get off home now straight away, if that's all right with you, Matt,' Marcia said in a business-like way. 'I'll get my report written and email a copy to you people here for your records. I'll make sure people hear of Mr and Mrs Cooks' little game, believe me. Those two will have a surprise when they show up at the tourist office in the morning saying they had to leave the place immediately, since we can prove that they slept here last night, dead rats or not.'

Annie looked horrified. 'You didn't find . . . ?'

Matt laughed. 'No way. The place is spotless. So are you going to return their lost property to them, Marcia?'

'Not me, or you either. I could hand it over to Bob for safe keeping — unofficially, I mean, since we know who owns it. He could put out a request on Radio Scilly, I suppose, for the owner to contact him.' She thought for a moment and her face lit up. 'Better still, Josh, why not hand it in to him at the police station first thing tomorrow and make it official? It will be on their records then.'

'Brilliant,' Lucy said.

'They'll get it back in due course,' Marcia continued, 'but they'll have to go to the police station to claim it, saying exactly where it was found and when. It was clear when we pulled back the covers that the bed had been slept in. There's our proof.'

Penny sprang up and gave Marcia a quick hug. 'So aren't you going to tell us what it is?'

Matt opened his closed fist, and there in the palm of his hand was a silver bracelet. He turned it over to show them the engraving inside.

Penny peered closer to read the inscription out loud. 'To my darling Sandy from her loving Rick.'

'Is it valuable?' Annie asked.

'Could be,' Matt replied.

'Valuable or not, I can see it's helpful to us,' Lucy said. 'Well done, Marcia. What would we do without you?'

Marcia gave her tinkling laugh, her face rosy with pleasure. 'I'm glad to be of any help I can, believe me. We can't do with dishonest people like that.' She declined any refreshment, and Matt didn't get any either, as he was driving her home.

What an afternoon. Please, no more

like that! Lucy thought. Annie's homesickness might well have been aggravated
by the events, but this evening when
Josh had run the two girls down to
Hugh Town to visit some of their new
friends, she had looked a great deal
more cheerful as they drove off.

But Josh still hadn't told Lucy what
was bothering him.

8

The first indication that Lucy was not alone was the appearance of a tall figure in a green jacket walking across the beach towards the start of the path that led up to Polwhenna. She was too far away to see who it was, but by the way he was striding out, she suspected it was Matt.

Lucy stood up and began to walk back along the path. She had reached the stone stile by the time he saw her. They met where the two paths crossed.

'I was coming to find you, Lucy,' he said. He was wearing walking boots now instead of the shoes he had on earlier. His auburn hair was slightly ruffled by the rising breeze.

'Is there any more news about the Cooks?' she said.

'Who?'

'The people who tried it on about Tamarisk.'

'Should there be?'

Lucy gave a little shrug. 'I couldn't help wondering.'

'Put it behind you, Lucy. You're not still worried about their ridiculous claims, are you?' He sounded concerned, but he was smiling.

'Why would anyone do something like that?'

'Maybe they changed their minds at the last minute and found somewhere down in Hugh Town they liked better. Near the shops? A sea view? Who knows? It happens sometimes.'

'To your parents?'

'They've had people not show up, but never anyone wanting a refund. But the Cooks will soon know they don't stand a chance. Look on the bright side, Lucy. There won't be much cleaning to do on the property next Saturday, will there? A morning off. Too bad I won't be here, or I'd have taken you off to one of the other islands for the day.'

Lucy felt surprisingly dismayed. 'You're going away?'

'Flying out tomorrow — a last-minute lecture tour starting off in Exeter. And while I'm there, they need someone to explain a few things to a new group starting up. I gather they want me to open their first event.'

'To raise money?'

'Is that such a bad thing?'

'It depends what it's for.'

He smiled. 'I won't tell you how important all this work is to the environment because I know I'll be wasting my breath.'

She looked at the sea, the sky and the distant islands. The beauty of it all was breathtaking. He sounded keen to be away, which felt depressing even though she knew he was only doing his job, just as she was doing hers here in helping out at Polwhenna because Miranda had decided to leave. The difference was that she was in a place she wanted to be. Maybe Matt would be feeling the same about his time off the islands.

'You'll still be here when I return?' he said.

She hesitated. All the time there was the thought that Miranda might come back as suddenly as she had left, and Lucy knew she must be prepared for that. 'I hope so,' she said.

Matt smiled. 'Let's walk.'

'I haven't been down on the beach yet this evening. I haven't seen the tide so far out either.'

'Then come with me.' He put out a hand to help her down the last stony part of the path, although he must have known she didn't need it. Her cheeks felt warm at his touch, and when he let go there was a faint sense of loss that disturbed her.

They walked to the far end of the beach and clambered round the corner on rocks that at any other time would have seemed tricky to negotiate. This evening Lucy found no difficulty, and Matt didn't try to help her again.

And now there was a different view,

with different islands across the hazy water. Or were they part of the ones she had already seen? It was hard to tell. It seemed important, suddenly, to work that out for herself, and to imprint them on her memory as if she would never see them again.

'Something wrong?' Matt asked.

She blinked. 'No, no. Nothing's wrong. It's so lovely, that's all. Which islands are we looking at now?'

'That's St Martin's straight across, and the Eastern Islands to the right.'

'They look intriguing.'

'I used to think that when I was a lad going out fishing with my Uncle Matthew, until . . .'

His silence seemed fraught with regret and he looked sad now. Lucy wished she knew why, but couldn't ask. To break the mood a little, she commented on the golden sands of the larger island she could see across the water, St Martin's. 'So beautiful,' she murmured. 'I shall go there one day.

'Yes, beautiful,' Matt murmured.

Penny had told Lucy that often there were evening events here in high season with reduced return fares from St Mary's that she and her friends took advantage of. Lucy thought about that now, and of how change could happen so unexpectedly. One moment tranquillity, the next popular music ringing out in the quiet air. And then tranquillity again until the next time.

They walked on, and the sand underfoot was as silvery white and soft as the beach they had left behind. On the summit of the steep overgrown ground bordering it was a stand of trees that looked surprisingly out of place.

Matt saw Lucy looking up at them. 'There's another tomb up there somewhere,' he said.

'One of the eighty?'

'Penny's told you that Scilly has the highest concentration of them in the UK?'

Lucy's face clouded. 'She was going to show me where the Iron Age village was, but we didn't have time. I had to get back to deal with those Cooks.'

He smiled at her kindly. 'Something to do another day, then.'

Of course he was right. He must think her an awful fool for harping on about them, and it was about time that she put the whole thing out of her mind as the others had appeared to do, even Josh. Marcia would make sure the owners of other establishments knew what had happened and to be on their guard. People would be routing for them. They weren't alone.

She took a deep breath and then smiled at Matt.

'That's better,' he said.

'How can you bear to leave all this, even for a short time?'

'All part of my work. It's good that support groups are starting up and making plans to visit the islands. All most encouraging.'

His work again, she thought; always there in his thoughts. Could he never let it go even for a second? 'I shall have to go back to Polwhenna soon,' she said. 'It's getting late.'

There was a moment of hesitation, and she saw an expression in his eyes that surprised her.

He indicated the rough ground at the top of the beach. 'We can get up here,' he said, 'and join the coastal path that will take us back. It's not too rough for you, I hope?'

He didn't wait for an answer, but led the way up through the overgrown vegetation on a path so steep and narrow it was almost invisible.

* * *

Afterwards, Matt wondered at his self-control down there on the beach when he had wanted to sweep Lucy into his arms to dispel that anxious look that had clouded her expression. The Cooks' ridiculous claims were hardly her fault, but she had obviously taken them to heart and was worrying unnecessarily. There were enough excellent reviews online to show that anything they came up with was vindictive and untrue.

Of course the islands needed all the good publicity they could get, and it was part of his job to see that they got it. An enormous amount of interest and support had been shown as soon as the reason for the steep decline in the numbers of nesting seabirds had become known. Peoples' imaginations had been caught as the programme for the extinction of the rats on St Agnes had gone ahead.

So Matt had been surprised at Lucy's reaction when he mentioned it. That she plainly considered him a murderer had upset him more than he let on. Now that the seabirds were beginning to return to the islands to breed, his heart was filled with joy. Scilly was the ideal home for them, with the rich surrounding seas for feeding. When he had tried to tell Lucy this before they parted near the entrance to Polwhenna, she had been unconvinced, and that was hurtful. His island home meant all the world to him. He loved the space, the freedom and the laid-back atmosphere. This was what the visitors loved, and what brought them back year after year.

He sighed as he put the last item in his hold-all ready for his departure tomorrow. This was *Prehistoric Scilly*, a second-hand book he'd picked up at the church craft fair yesterday. He had only looked in as a mark of support and had poked about among the books on the stall under the far window because he was sorry for Janey Baxter, a thin wisp of a girl who looked half-frozen to death.

'That draught's a killer,' he had told her. 'Shall I help you lift your table to a better position?'

But she had shaken her head and he hadn't pressed the matter. Instead he had picked up this book and handed over twice the amount of money she asked for. His reward was her sudden smile and a book that was proving to be surprisingly interesting. No harm in adding to his knowledge on the subject, even if he'd teased Penny more than once for her obsession with it.

*   *   *

The Cook fiasco seemed to have strengthened something in Josh. He came down to breakfast next day wearing a white T-shirt so new that the creases where it had been folded were still apparent. He looked brighter than normal, too, and Tanya's look of approval made Lucy smile.

'I think,' he said, his voice solemn, 'that a barbecue evening would be a good idea.'

'Here?' Annie said.

'We always had them once a week or so for the guests, weather permitting, throughout the summer.'

'But then why . . . ?' Tanya began.

'Brilliant idea,' Lucy said quickly.

'We can invite others, too, for the first one.'

'Even better.'

'So when?' Annie said.

'Wednesday.'

'That soon?'

'I thought you Australians were used to barbies?'

Tanya snorted.

Annie twisted a strand of her long fair hair. 'Ace,' she said. 'We can do it.'

'I'll make a list,' Lucy said, getting up.

'Wednesday,' Josh repeated. 'Six o'clock. A swim first for anyone who wants to. That suit you girls?'

Annie's eyes sparkled. 'For us too?'

'Didn't I just say so? A special event, our barbecue. We'll make it a good one.'

'I'll need new bathers,' Annie said.

'I'll run you girls down to town this afternoon,' Josh said.

Tanya looked interested. 'And you'll bring us back again?'

'One hour?'

'You're on.' He looked round the kitchen, his brow furrowed. 'There's an extra stock of china and utensils here somewhere.'

'I'll stay here while you go and get that sorted out,' Lucy said, already busy writing at the work unit.

'You know where to look?'

She smiled. 'I'll find it.'

He nodded and got up.

* * *

Marcia phoned early in the afternoon to say that Sandy and Rick Cook's blustering demands had got them nowhere. 'I pointed out that I had photographic evidence with witnesses that they were lying, and that my word was more likely to be believed than theirs. Bullies, the pair of them, and easily deflated.'

'And the bracelet?' Lucy asked.

'Not a word.'

Lucy had soon suspected that Marcia's comfortable figure and friendly smile disguised a determined character that was a match for the likes of the Cooks. It was a relief that she was right. 'We're so grateful to you, Marcia,' she said. 'You'll come to the barbecue we're having, won't you?'

'On Wednesday evening?'

'You know about it?'

'I'll bring something to help out.'

Lucy knew it was no use protesting. 'Thanks, Marcia. We look forward to seeing you.'

But the weather had other ideas. The rain started at breakfast time and looked settled in for the day. Fortunately there was plenty of room in the freezer for the supplies of fresh meat Annie said they needed. Once the go-ahead came and it was defrosted, it wouldn't take them long to make the burgers and kebabs. Josh had insisted on plenty of sausages, and there were lamb chops too. Lucy had, with difficulty, made room for the packets of bacon. The lettuce, rocket and tomatoes in the vegetable garden could stay where they were for the time being.

★　★　★

Lucy got up from the computer in the study on Wednesday morning to gaze out of the window at the trees bending with the fury of the wind. She found it impossible to believe that the sky would ever be blue again, or the birds would sing. The planes weren't flying this morning either, and no wonder.

She thought briefly of the Manx shearwaters in their nesting burrows on the outer islands. And what were the others Matt was particularly interested in? Terns, stormy petrels? No doubt they could take care of themselves in this weather. Humans were best indoors.

There was a crash from the direction of the kitchen some time later, and Lucy was up and dashing downstairs two steps at a time.

Annie was lying on the floor, surrounded by tins and packets that had shed their contents round her in a mass of rice and a mist of flour. She looked up, white-faced. 'I'm okay.'

'You look like you're in the middle of

a snowstorm.' The steps were semi-collapsed against the cupboard. Lucy righted them and helped Annie up.

'My ankle, that's all.'

Lucy pulled a chair forward for her to sit down. 'You're in a lot of pain, Annie, I know you are. And look how much it's swollen.' She knelt down on the floury floor and took the ankle in her hands. Gentle as she was, she felt the involuntary tremble, and this decided her. 'The minor injuries clinic for you.'

'No, really.'

'No argument, Annie.'

The rain had eased off a little, but they were still wet by the time Lucy had helped Annie into the back of the car. A scribbled note left on the kitchen table to Josh and Tanya would suffice for the moment. She would phone Polwhenna later.

9

It seemed best to drive Annie to the kitchen entrance on their return, as there were no steps here to negotiate. Once out of the car, and with the crutch she had been given, Annie managed to get herself to the door without help.

Lucy held it open for her. Inside, Josh looked up from the letter he was reading. The note she had written was still on the table, opened out and obviously read.

'Thanks for phoning,' he said. 'I'm glad it was no worse.' He pulled out a chair for Annie, and Lucy hung their discarded jackets over two of the chairs near the Aga to dry.

She glanced round at the clean and tidy kitchen. Not a vestige of spilled rice and flour was there. 'You did all this?'

Josh looked perplexed. 'All what?'

'Cleaned it. Everything.'

She saw now that there were neatly written labels on all the doors with the contents listed. Amazing. She went closer to look. Behind her she heard Josh asking Annie all the details of her fall and checking that the steps were not faulty.

'I was reaching too far,' Annie said. 'I slipped. Lucy was great.'

'And it's a sprain? No bones broken? You did the right thing, Lucy. I'm sorry I wasn't here.' He looked down at the paper in his hand, folded it and put it in the letter rack on the worktop by the door into the hall. 'I'll deal with that later. Coffee? I think we could do with it.' He made it swiftly and sat down at the table with the girls.

'The place was a tip, Josh,' Annie said. 'I thought I'd have to see to it when we got back.'

Lucy laughed. 'It's good that the kitchen fairy got to work while we were away.'

'Tanya, of course.' Annie was sure of that.

Josh nodded. 'Of course.' He got up to make more coffee for her. The line of his back as he stood there waiting for the kettle to boil looked dejected, and Lucy thought of the letter he had been reading so intently when she had helped Annie into the kitchen. There was something going on here she didn't quite understand. Annie's ankle was sprained, and with rest and a bit of luck would be healed in a few days. There was nothing here that should cause Josh such deep concern.

Lucy was reminded, suddenly, of a long-ago visit to Polwhenna when, in this very kitchen, his mother — her aunt Jane — had scolded her young son for not doing something or other, and poured scorn on him for ignoring the note she had left for him. Even as a child, it had seemed to Lucy an unfair attack, and she had felt a rush of sympathy for Josh. Neither he nor his mother were aware of her presence, and

133

she had crept out into the sunshine of the garden, glad to escape the heavy atmosphere.

Lucy drank her coffee thoughtfully, willing Josh to forget whatever it was that was troubling him now. The hot drink had brought the colour back into Annie's cheeks, and her eyes were bright.

Lucy smiled at her. 'Better now?'

'Oh yes.'

'But what happened to Tanya?'

'She wasn't well. She went up to her room.'

Lucy sprang up. 'I'd better investigate.'

She knocked gently on the door the girls shared and was relieved at the immediate response. As she opened the door, the curtains fluttered at the open window. The room felt cold.

'Tanya?'

She was lying on the bed nearest the window with her hands behind her head. She sat up straight when she saw Lucy. 'Anything wrong?'

Lucy expected scorn from Tanya at her friend's ineptitude, but there was nothing. Instead she lay back on her pillow again. Lucy hadn't seen Tanya like this before and it was worrying. 'Are you all right?' she asked the girl.

'Just needed a rest, that's all. I'm allowed that, aren't I? What a mess down there. Did you see my labels on the cupboards?'

'You did them? They're brilliant. What gave you the idea?'

Tanya's flush at the praise made her look softer and more vulnerable, and for the first time Lucy felt closer to her. 'I could bring you up something on a tray if you're not feeling too good.'

'I don't want any food. The barbie . . . '

Lucy glanced out of the window at the trees bowed down with rain. 'Not today. It's postponed. 'I'll get you a drink then.'

'Ace.'

Josh and Annie were still in the kitchen when Lucy went downstairs, and her cousin had got the makings of a simple meal out on the worktop. After they'd eaten, he indicated that he wanted a word with Lucy in the sitting room, and she was glad to go with him. They stood together at the large bay window that gave a view of the drive and the front gate that, as usual, stood open.

'So Tanya cleaned up the mess in the kitchen while we were away,' Lucy said.

'Mmm.'

She looked at him swiftly, immediately suspicious. 'You did that?'

'I thought there'd been some sort of row and she'd flounced off. Best to get it cleaned up before you brought Annie back. I'm used to things like that.'

'Ah.'

He flushed, obviously aware that he had let out more than he intended. 'But Tanya was there,' he said, 'at the end. She helped me, you see. But then she went off and I took no notice. I was thinking of other things.'

Lucy, taking advantage of the moment,

said that she had noticed his recent dejection and asked if there was anything she could do to help.

He picked up a paperweight from the windowsill and pursed his lips at the discolouration of the paint it left behind. 'I'll have to do something about that.' He frowned. 'The whole room needs redecorating. Miranda . . . '

'Miranda?'

'She wrote again. A longer letter this time. She's heard that we're getting on all right at Polwhenna. That's what she wants.'

Lucy waited. This was news indeed. Josh had obviously been totally lost at the beginning, and she had done her very best to make things easy for him with the help of Tanya and Annie. But now Annie was out of action, and possibly Tanya as well. She had been asleep when Lucy had taken up a glass of barley water for her. In an hour she would check on the girl again.

She glanced at Josh and saw that he was smiling at the paperweight he was holding. He held it up the light, and a flicker of emerging sunlight reflected blue and silver flecks onto the discoloured paintwork. 'A present from Miranda,' he said. 'Our fifth wedding anniversary. I think there could be a chance we could make a go of it again if she sees I'm working all out for this place.' He looked up at Lucy, his expression hopeful.

She felt a rush of affection for this cousin of hers who had been so kind to her when she was a little girl. She smiled, but didn't point out that she knew nothing of why Miranda had left the islands in the first place and so wasn't in a position to comment.

'Will you help me, Lucy?'

Her reaction was instantaneous. 'Of course I will. We'll go for a lovely barbecue on Friday with the present tenants, who'll be happy and wanting to book again for next year.'

'A lovely barbecue,' Josh said, his eyes shining. 'That'll please Miranda.'

Two days to do what needed to be

done. Well, why not? Even with Annie and possibly Tanya out of action. Lucy hoped that Marcia was right about anyone who turned up, other than their present guests, bringing something suitable for the feast with them. She smiled. 'You're on.'

Josh replaced the paperweight on the windowsill. He looked happier now, his mouth curving into a smile. Lucy was glad to see it, but her heart felt heavy as she thought of having to leave all this and go back home soon. Still, there would be a week or two yet before she needed to book her return passage, and she would make the most of the time. There was even the chance that Matt would be back in time to come to their barbecue, and that thought was cheering.

* * *

He was more than a kitten really, Lucy thought. More of a teenage cat, attracted by the chatter and the lights;

or, more likely, the smell of the sausages and chops sizzling on the barbecue. But where had he come from? He was completely black, and wearing a yellow collar. He looked in fine condition as he purred round her ankles. She picked him up.

'So who are you?' she murmured. His fur was warm and soft as she stroked him. She thought of the tiny kitten that, when she was five years old, she had thought was a present for her when she found him in the back garden of their temporary Putney home. Her disappointment had been acute when his owner had appeared and borne him off. Worse was discovering a few months later that a litter of newborn kittens had been drowned in a bucket of water by that same owner. The anguish she had felt then swept over her briefly now.

But this little charmer surely had a loving owner, maybe someone present at their barbecue this evening. Lucy kissed the top of his head and put him down. He followed her as she moved towards the barbecue, still purring loudly. She was smiling as she picked up a paper plate. Josh, seeing her, scraped up the last of the lamb chops.

'You're in luck, Lucy,' he said. He looked totally relaxed as he stood there in his long white apron. 'Bacon, sausages? No beef burgers or kebabs left, I'm afraid.'

'I thought there might not be anything,' she said. A wave of relief swept over her that things were going well. Tanya was back in action, thank goodness, and all this week's tenants were here having the time of their lives. She was glad to see that Simon Hartley, over by the picnic table where Annie was sitting, was obviously enjoying himself. He was due to leave tomorrow after his fortnight's holiday and Lucy would be sorry to see him go. So would the girls, she knew. But that was life in the holiday business.

There were other people too, all looking completely at home. They had been greeted by Penny, who had suggested she help out. She was talking with animation to Marcia. Now, seeing Lucy, she gave her a cheerful wave. 'Be with you in a minute,' she called.

Lucy, standing where she was, ate the food on her plate and then helped herself to more: salad this time, and a hunk of baguette someone had brought. What a difference stoking up with food did for her well-being.

She looked round for the teenage kitten. Not the slightest sound of purring now. He'd vanished. Could she just have imagined him? She had been light-headed with hunger, after all.

She shook herself mentally. Time for a bit of socialising, now that her responsibilities for making the evening a success for their tenants was over. Josh was obviously pleased. He was waving his spatula in the air and talking to a girl Lucy didn't know. He looked more animated than she had seen for a long time, probably hoping their success would get back to Miranda. Ah well, no use worrying about her now.

'Why the frown?'

Startled, Lucy looked up and smiled at Penny. 'Any coffee left?'

'I'll get us some.'

Lucy seated herself on the opposite side of the picnic table occupied by Annie and Simon. Penny, joining her a few moments later, gave him a sharp glance and made to move away.

'Don't mind me,' he said. He got up and patted Annie on the shoulder. 'Glad your ankle's well on the mend. Anyway, I'm off. People to see.'

Annie's eyes followed him as he walked away. 'He means Tanya,' she said, her voice bleak.

'Tanya? But I thought . . . ' Lucy broke off at a stir in the gap in the hedge, and two people appeared, each remonstrating with the other. They looked a little awkward as they came into the barbecue area, both silent now. Sandy and Rick Cook! Whoever would have thought it?

She sprang up. 'Can I help you?'

143

There was a brief lull in the surrounding chatter, and in that time Lucy was aware that the atmosphere had changed a little.

'I'll find Marcia,' Penny said, and disappeared.

Josh, still on duty at his post, appeared to have noticed nothing, and Marcia and Dan were keeping well out of it.

Lucy stepped towards the Cooks and smiled. 'So you didn't head for the mainland after all?'

She saw that Sandy Cook's eyes were red and her lips were trembling. 'Well no, I . . . '

Technically they were still their tenants. Morally . . . well, that was a different matter. But a public row must be avoided at all costs.

10

Lucy, struggling to keep calm and deal with the situation with all the confidence at her command, indicated the picnic table where Annie still sat. The chatter started again now, and under its cover she said, 'Please come over here with me. Are you hungry? There's still some food left. Let me get you some.'

Rick cleared his throat. He was wearing, like his wife, tight white jeans topped with a black T-shirt. Sandy had tied a patterned scarf round her throat, and she used one end of it now to dab at her eyes. 'I'm hungry,' she murmured.

Rick turned on her. 'Hungry at a time like this? Have some sense. It's not food we've come for.'

'But . . . ' Lucy said, surprised, ' . . . we want people to be hungry when they come to our barbecues.' She felt proud of sounding so genuine, and was rewarded by an embarrassed flush on Rick Cook's cheeks. He tried to pull away from Sandy's grip but she was holding on tightly.

Lucy went at once, filled a plate with as much as she could find, and brought it back.

'You're kind,' Sandy said in wonder as she took it from her. 'Look, Rick, there's plenty here for both of us.' She sat down at the picnic table and held the plate towards him. Shamefacedly, he sat down too.

'You're very welcome,' Lucy said.

Annie had said nothing, but she looked astonished. As well she might, Lucy thought as she squashed in beside her. She hoped that by acting in this way, Rick would continue to feel as uncomfortable as Sandy at their unexpected reception. It was nothing more than they deserved, and it was fun doing it, but she mustn't get carried away.

'We're here to collect some lost

property,' Rick said abruptly.

'Oh?' Lucy said innocently.

'It's my bracelet,' Sandy explained, her voice trembling. 'It's special, you see.'

'And where did you drop it?'

'You must have found it.' Rick sounded angry now.

'We found something when we remade the bed.'

Sandy's face lit up. 'Oh, thank you. That's great.'

'I'm sure it will be all right,' Lucy said in a soothing tone. 'If the bracelet really is yours.'

'It is,' Sandy said. 'I put it there, under the pillow.'

'So you placed it there for safe keeping when you went to bed?'

A growl started in Rick's throat. 'But we didn't . . . ' Sandy broke off and looked guiltily at him. He glared back at her. 'What's all this nonsense about?' he demanded. 'Did you find it or didn't you? Tell me that.'

Lucy ignored him. 'And when you

woke next morning, Sandy . . . ' she said, ' . . . that would be Sunday, wouldn't it? You forgot about it?'

Sandy hesitated, and the silence seemed to last forever. Annie moved a little in her seat, and from the corner of her eye Lucy saw Penny coming back. 'Everything all right?' Penny called.

Before she reached them, Sandy spoke urgently. 'Yes, it's mine.'

Rick got to his feet, scowling. 'So where is it now?'

'Josh handed it in to the police,' Lucy said.

'Police?' echoed Sandy, alarmed. She got up too, and stood close to her husband.

'At the police station,' Lucy confirmed.

'The police station?'

'You can go along there first thing in the morning.' Sandy's face was a picture, and Lucy bit back a giggle. 'To ask about lost property,' she said, 'that's all. You haven't anything else to worry, about have you?'

'Oh.'

Lucy felt something soft rubbing against her ankles. She looked down and saw the kitten. 'Oh,' she said in delight. He purred loudly as she picked him up.

'A cat?' said Rick in horror. He cringed away, nearly falling over the bench end.

'Only a little one,' Lucy said, stroking the soft fur.

'He's sweet,' Sandy murmured. 'What's his name?' She tried to move closer to Lucy but her husband yanked her back towards him.

'We're out of here, Sandy.'

'But I . . . '

Lucy could see, by Rick's change of colour, that something was wrong. For a moment he seemed unable to move.

'Nero won't hurt you, Mr Cook,' said Annie. She smiled sweetly up at him and patted the bench at her side. 'Come and sit down by me. We don't want you to go, do we, Lucy?'

She was learning fast, Lucy thought.

Nero — where had that come from?

But Rick had other ideas. He dragged Sandy off through the gap in the hedge. Penny sank down beside Annie, shaking with mirth.

Lucy felt an instant's sympathy. She knew about irrational fears and phobias. Spiders, yuck! But who could compare a kitten with a spider? Kittens were soft and warm and purring. She could never hurt a kitten; but then she wouldn't kill a spider either, although many other people would for no reason other than that they didn't like them. She frowned a little. There was something niggling her thoughts here, but now was not the time to work out what it was.

There was another movement among a group of people beginning to say their farewells, and Matt's tall figure emerged from among them. He came straight across to the picnic table.

'Just in time to help with the clearing up,' Penny said.

'A lift home — wasn't that the idea,

little sister? You knew I might be late back this evening.'

'You missed the exciting bit. Lucy saw them off good and proper.'

Matt smiled round at them all. 'From the look of things, it's just as well. I met those Cooks of yours escaping in good order.'

Lucy held up the little cat. 'Meet Nero, the star of the show.'

He took the animal from her and looked at him closely. 'I've seen you before, haven't I? Your yellow collar's a giveaway.'

'You know him?'

'I don't know how he got himself here from Old Town. I'm almost sure he belongs to an elderly couple there. Should I go and check? I know they keep late hours.'

'You'd take her little cat away from Lucy?' Penny said in an accusing tone. 'How cruel is that?'

'He's not mine,' Lucy said, 'that's why.' She got up and gave him a last loving stroke.

Matt gave her a look of approval. 'Like to come too, Lucy? He'll need someone to hold him in the car.'

Her heart leapt. 'Yes, please.' A little more time with Nero. Great. And with Matt too. She felt herself flush with pleasure.

Most people had left now, and Matt's car was parked in a convenient spot. The interior smelt slightly of seaweed — but how could that be? He was wearing smarter clothes than she had seen him in before: a pale blue open-neck shirt and new chinos, by the look of them. Not the sort of gear to go collecting seaweed on the beaches. She wrinkled her nose.

He smiled at her. 'What's wrong?'

'It odd,' she said. 'Why is there a whiff of seaweed in here?'

'It's simple. I took delivery of this vehicle in Penzance on Monday and had it shipped over here. A Honda Civic. D'you like it?'

There was such pride in his voice that it seemed churlish of her to have raised the slightest criticism. 'It looks new.'

'Second-hand but in tip-top condition.'

Lucy fastened her seatbelt. 'So do all Hondas come complete with a dashing whiff of seaweed, or is it only the ones heading for the islands?'

Matt laughed as he put the car into gear. 'The previous owner was a market gardener. He must have carried a bag or two of fertiliser. Either that, or he liked the scent. Any sign of a seaweed-scented car freshener dangling anywhere?'

She laughed. 'Problem solved.'

'You like solving problems?'

'I like to know the ins and outs of things. Yes, that's true.'

Nero's purrs seemed even louder as they set off.

'Just listen to your little cat,' Matt said.

Lucy glanced at him. 'Mine? I wish.'

'You seem fond of animals. All animals?'

For a moment Lucy didn't respond. It wasn't hard to see where this was going, and she didn't feel like a discussion about it now. She stifled a yawn. 'Something like that.'

They were travelling down the road to Old Town. She didn't often come this way, and for the first time glimpsed the notice pinned to a board near the entrance to the farm on the corner. But they were past it before she could read what it said.

'Accommodation being offered,' Matt said, seeing the twist of her head. 'The son's just got married and the daughter-in-law is keen to set something up. Good luck to her.'

'Do you know everything that happens on these islands?' Lucy said, marvelling.

Matt laughed. 'I know that the Littlewoods at Sea View have a small black cat very like that purring object in your lap wearing a yellow collar. Are you astonished that I managed to put two and two together?'

'So I've no hope of keeping him?'

He shot her an amused glance. 'As much as the islands becoming one land mass again and joining up with the mainland.'

'Not too good a chance, then. But how did he get as far as Polwhenna?'

'Climbed unseen into someone's parked car, perhaps. Who knows? Ah, here we are now.' He drew up outside a stone cottage that looked solidly comfortable in its strip of front garden full of the shiny green thrusting leaves Lucy recognised as agapanthus.

The door flew open as soon as Matt tapped gently on it. Lucy had expected an elderly lady bent double over her walking stick mourning for her lost cat. Instead, here was a jolly-looking person with blue eyes and white hair cut short to her head who exclaimed in delight at seeing them.

'Matt!' she exclaimed.

He gave her a quick hug. 'Barbara! And I've brought Lucy from Polwhenna, and someone else too that you may have been missing.'

'Oh!' Her relief was plain to see. She held the kitten to her and buried her face in his fur as he purred with delight. When she looked up again, Lucy saw the tears of relief in her eyes. Her own filled in sympathy and she wiped them away with her hand, hoping no one had noticed.

'We've been looking everywhere,' Barbara said. 'Oh you naughty boy, Rio. Where have you been all this time?'

Lucy smiled. So that was his name — Rio. And not so different-sounding from Nero. Annie had been inspired when she thought of it.

The next moment she was being greeted herself, though not in such an exuberant manner. 'Hello, Lucy my dear. Come in, both of you. Close the door, Matt.'

He stooped to follow the others along a narrow passage smelling of lavender, through a surprisingly large, brightly lit kitchen, and into an adjoining smaller room with easy chairs facing a large television set. Edward Littlewood, taller even than Matt, got to his feet, zapping the TV into black silence.

'Look who's come home again, Edward. I'm so thrilled to see the little monkey.'

Her husband cleared his throat as he took the kitten from her, stroked him and then placed him on the floor. 'And brought someone with him, I see.'

Introductions were made. Edward Littlewood's hand felt icy, but in his quiet way he was as welcoming as his wife. They both pressed Matt and Lucy to stay and join them in a late-night drink, but that wasn't possible, Matt said. 'We're due back at Polwhenna, I'm afraid. My sister will be champing at the bit, wanting a lift home. Another time, perhaps.'

'Of course,' Barbara said, her voice warm. 'And please, Lucy, feel free to visit this little monster whenever you like. I can see how fond of him you are.'

Lucy, thanking her, gave Rio a last pat and then followed Matt to the door.

157

11

'But we're not going the right way,' Lucy said as they set off once more. Instead of returning the way they had come, Matt had turned right, and they were now travelling towards Hugh Town.

'You've noticed?'

'Always observant, that's me. One of my rare talents.'

'I wouldn't say that.'

She smiled. Now what exactly did that mean? Maybe he thought she was endowed with many talents. Mmn, nice thought, but she wouldn't risk asking.

'D'you mind a different route?' he asked.

She turned to smile at him. 'I'd only mind if you're planning to press-gang me into your family boat and whisk me off to a far distant island.'

'Would that be so bad?'

'It would be at this time of night.'

'An earlier time of day?'

'Maybe.'

'I might hold you to that.'

She could tell by his tone of voice that he was smiling too. The feeling that she was being looked after was pleasant, and she was glad they had come round this way because it meant being in Matt's company for a little longer.

'There's something I'd like you to see,' he said.

They had reached Hugh Town now and were turning right into the main road to go back to Polwhenna. Minutes later, Matt turned into the side road that Lucy knew led to Pengarth Beach and his parents' home. The headlights picked out the banks of the narrow lane. He drove slowly and pulled up on the patch of grass between the house and the beach.

'You've forgotten I'm not Penny,' Lucy accused, laughing. 'She's back at Polwhenna — remember, waiting for a lift home?'

He pulled on the handbrake. 'Mixing you up with my sister is one thing I'd never do.'

'But why are we here?'

He opened his door. 'Come on. I hope we'll see.'

The air felt surprisingly balmy now, and the sea in this sheltered bay was only slightly ruffled with a sheen of silver catching the tips of the tiny waves. Lucy realised suddenly that the wind had dropped. 'It's beautiful here,' she murmured.

'Look over there, Lucy!'

In the light of the car's headlights, she could pick out a dark shape on the other side of the beach. Matt pulled out a torch and flicked on the light. 'My latest acquisition,' he said.

'A boat?'

'My very own.'

They moved towards it across sand that was soft to the feet. Matt gave an exclamation of pleasure when they reached the boat, and Lucy could feel his pride in the way he stood with one hand lightly on the side. 'I hoped it'd arrived,' he said. 'The landing craft was due to come today. My plane was delayed, you see, and I went straight to our headquarters to make a report on the latest fundraising. I thought I'd miss your barbecue if I didn't hurry. There wasn't time to check down here first.'

'Penny didn't say a word?'

'She wouldn't have known the boat was mine.'

'And then you spent time taking Rio back to his owners before you came here!' Lucy marvelled that he hadn't shown by a flicker of impatience that there was something of this importance waiting for him here. How many other men would have done the same? she wondered. Not many — and not many women either, she suspected. She certainly wouldn't have been able to keep quiet about it herself.

Matt smiled. 'Taking poor Rio home to Barbara and Edward was one way to ensure I could show you *Free Spirit* before anyone else.'

Lucy hesitated at the implications of his words, not knowing how to respond. She longed, suddenly, to be back in her room at Polwhenna with time to think about it. And yet at the same time she wanted to be here with Matt on this quiet darkened beach, and for this moment never to end. But his boat was named *Free Spirit*, and a free spirit allowed for no compromise. How could she be happy with someone who held such different views about important issues?

She took a deep breath. '*Free Spirit*,' she said reflectively. 'A beautiful name.'

'A beautiful concept,' Matt agreed.

There was silence. Invisible small waves lapped the edge of the sand, and their sound seemed to roar in Lucy's ears. She was tired, so dreadfully tired.

And now there were other people here too. 'You didn't tell me it was yours, Matt!' Lucy would have recognised her friend's ringing tones anywhere as Penny came leaping down the beach

162

towards them. She hadn't been aware of the arrival of Marcia's car, but now in the beam of Dan's torch she recognised her and her brother.

Dan shone his light at *Free Spirit* and murmured in approval, while his sister said that giving Penny a lift home was no trouble, especially as it meant seeing this beauty.

'So you didn't know it was here, Matt?' Penny said. She sounded incredulous. 'You really had no idea?'

'Not until I came to check just now.'

'So we won't be able to drag you away from it just yet then?' Marcia said.

'I'll be back after I've taken Lucy home.'

Marcia laughed. 'We'll leave you to it in that case. Dan?'

He yawned. 'I'm for bed.'

'I'll see it in the morning,' Penny said, yawning too. 'I hope there's going to be an official launch.'

'Tomorrow afternoon,' Matt confirmed. 'Three o'clock.' But Marcia and Dan were already trudging up the beach, dark shadows now. With a wave to Lucy, Penny followed them.

'You'll join us then, Lucy?' said Matt.

'Saturday's a busy day.'

'Josh could make an exception and give you the afternoon off.'

She hesitated. 'I . . . I don't know. I must find out what his plans are.' She felt drained by all the emotion of the evening. It had been a long day. She yawned as if she didn't care one way or the other, and yet he must know she would like to be with him.

Matt must have realised this, because he indicated they should leave the beach too. At Polwhenna he dropped her at the gate and was off at once. More than likely though the lure of his new possession was pulling him back to Pengarth.

★　★　★

Next day the changeover went well. Simon Hartley, promising to return to Scilly just as soon as he could, left soon

164

after nine. The occupants of Tamarisk took a little longer, but by eleven o'clock Tanya and Annie were at work on the cleaning.

The weather was kind too, the gentle breeze teasing the few clouds across a sky of deep cobalt-blue. A perfect drying day, Lucy thought as she pegged the last of the sheets on the line.

The lawnmower in the background was a soothing summer sound that she loved. That and the murmur of bees in the purple buddleia by the kitchen wall. And the birdsong everywhere in the garden, and the waves breaking on the shore.

She wondered what Matt was doing this morning if the launch wasn't until the afternoon. Maybe he had work to do . . . killing more rats? But no, she was being paranoid. His job now involved gaining publicity and support for all the work they were doing on the islands, as well as checking the status quo.

Lucy thought suddenly of Nero/Rio,

and that was strange. His home was in New Town, not up here at Polwhenna, even though the clever little thing had somehow got himself here yesterday all by himself. Maybe she should accept his owners' invitation to drop in and see him when she had some spare time.

Tanya and Annie had plans for the afternoon that involved a lift down to Hugh Town immediately after an early lunch. Standing at the sink with the washing-up and feeling a little like Cinderella, Lucy watched them go. Josh had promised to come straight back for the arrival of the first of their new tenants so that they could greet them together. This was an improvement on a week ago, when he had left the welcoming to her and had seemed to skulk in the background as if he was of no importance to the newcomers. When they came across him in the garden later on, they weren't aware of who he was.

'The new people aren't arriving until two at the earliest,' Josh said. 'Take some time off now, Lucy, why don't you. I'll be back in ten minutes.'

'I've time enough to walk down to the beach and back?'

'Plenty. And long enough to linger there, too.'

A breath of sea air would be welcome, she thought as she set out. And so would a few moments away from Polwhenna and her duties. The tide was on its way out, and the rounded boulders between the beach and Carn Island glittered in the sunshine. A family of four and a sprightly young dog appeared as if from nowhere and settled themselves down for an afternoon of sunbathing. They obviously weren't interested in Lucy, but she wanted to be quite alone anyway, so she set off further round to the left where she had previously walked with Matt. Here she settled herself against a prominent rock and looked out to the Eastern Isles.

She loved this place, and Josh did too. She had always known how much it meant to him. He was trying hard to make a success of Polwhenna in Miranda's absence, and Lucy had promised to help him all she could. She didn't know then that Miranda wanted something more than common courtesy from him: something concrete that would prove to her that his heart was in this business they had worked on together, and that his lethargy wasn't indicative of the state of their marriage, before she would consider returning to Scilly.

And so Josh was trying hard to do what she wanted. The successful barbecue was a start of course, but not really enough. He needed to think up something unique that Polwhenna had to offer and to put it into practice.

Lucy picked a piece of grass and chewed the end of the stalk. No one could describe Josh as being a man of ideas, and it was unfair of Miranda to set this test and expect the impossible. Lucy hated unfairness, especially when it involved Josh, who didn't deserve it.

But the task wasn't impossible if there was someone like herself to help him. Secret Haven, the half-finished property on the other side of the lawn, seemed not to have been touched since the day Miranda left. It would make good sense for it to be lived in all through the year, not just the summer months. She would suggest it at once and insist that Josh agree. They could advertise for a tenant who would act as a caretaker on occasion so that Josh and Miranda were free to leave the island sometimes during the quiet season. Brilliant!

Lucy's mind soared with the possibilities. She sprang up, wanting to tell Josh immediately. By the time she had clambered back across the rocks to the beach, she had made so many plans she felt she would burst.

But wait a minute! Breathing hard, she made herself stand still and think of the consequences. Miranda wouldn't want her here, that was certain. She would have to leave and return to her job in Truro and take up her life there helping Angus to clear the stock of his fading business.

And Matt? But she mustn't think of him. Her decision was made, and there was no turning away from it. Josh needed all the help she could give. It was what she had come here to do. And then Miranda would come home again and make him happy.

More soberly now, Lucy walked slowly across the beach and up the track. Soon she returned to Polwhenna, and with the key of Secret Haven in her hand, she crossed the lawn to take a look at it. She hadn't been inside the property since Josh had shown her round so proudly on the day of her arrival. 'All Miranda's work,' he had told her.

Yes, and that was obviously part of the trouble. His interest at the time must have been nil. But not from now on, Lucy thought, resolving to note down everything that still needed to be done and insist on Josh getting to grips with it.

170

She propped the door open with a handy stone and went inside to a room where a hint of new paint still lingered. The bedroom smelt arid and dusty. With the window wide open for fresh air, she stood with her back to it and looked critically at the unpainted walls and half-laid floor.

This was a nice little place; it was a shame that Josh had apparently lost interest in it. What was he thinking of, not to have completed it before? Not of Miranda's needs, that was for sure. But he would be now. There must be some action as soon as he got back from town! He wouldn't know what had hit him.

His car was just pulling into the drive when Lucy got back to the house, followed almost instantly by a taxi with the first of the new arrivals.

* * *

'You didn't tell me there was some-where else you should be this afternoon,

Lucy,' Josh said. They had greeted Mr and Mrs Woodcock together, and their new tenants were delighted with all that Tamarisk had to offer.

'I don't care if it rains all week; we'll be happy enough sitting in here looking out at the beautiful garden,' Marnie Woodcock had enthused.

Lucy basked in her praise, and even Josh looked pleased. He had immediately offered to show her husband round the garden, and they were gone so long that Lucy had plenty of time to tell Mrs Woodcock about some of the amenities the islands had to offer.

Now she and Josh were walking back to the house. He paused to break off a piece of overhanging scented honeysuckle.

'Oh?' Lucy said in response to his question.

'I met Barbara Littlewood in town.'

Lucy's mind immediately flew to the little cat. 'Rio's mum?'

Josh looked perplexed. 'What d'you mean?' He shrugged. 'The Littlewoods are going off to the Eastern Isles in the new boat belonging to the Hendersons, and you're supposed to be on its maiden voyage too.'

'It's Matt's own boat,' Lucy said. 'It belongs to him.'

'Even so. But you'll have to be quick. My car's out; I'll drive you. My jacket's in it — you can take that. Come on, Lucy — what are you waiting for?'

He took hold of her arm, and the next moment she was being driven off by a masterful Josh she hardly recognised. This was a change indeed. She lay back in her seat for a moment, pleased that at last he was coming to his senses. Then, her seatbelt tightening, she sat upright. This wasn't quite the action she wanted from him.

'Josh, please stop!'

'What's wrong?' He drew into the side of the road and did as she said. He looked so alarmed that she spoke quickly.

'I need you to promise me something, Josh. It's important. Miranda — '

'Miranda?'

'Secret Haven. We need to get it up and running. It was her wish.'

'You want me to work on it?'

His surprise was so genuine that it enraged her. She spilled out her idea for the place at such a rush she was breathless. 'Do it, Josh, just do it!'

'What, now?'

'Promise me.'

'And then you'll let me drive you the rest of the way before it's too late?'

'No, I want to go back.'

'You deserve some time off, Lucy. Don't be stupid.'

'But Josh, you don't understand. I — '

'All right. Secret Haven. I promise.' And with that he started the car again, and they were off.

It would be useless, Lucy decided, to tell him that she didn't want to be a captive audience on one of Matt's bird cruises, even if it was in his new boat that he was trying out for the first time. Josh would think she had taken leave of her senses, knowing how interested her family had always been in the natural world. She was still struggling with the concept that she might have been wrong in her condemnation of the work Matt had been involved in and didn't want any pressure at this moment. She wished she could have talked to her father to get his views, but he was on the other side of the world and was not due home for some time. Someone else's opinion might clear her head a little, someone who was removed from all this and wouldn't necessarily have their own agenda.

Moments later they arrived. *Free Spirit* was floating gently close to shore, and seated in the bows were Barbara and Edward Littlewood, the only two people Lucy recognised apart from Matt himself and Penny, who were both knee-deep in the water holding the boat in position. It was clear that the others had only just boarded.

Seeing Lucy, Barbara gave a wave.

There was nothing else for it, so Lucy removed her trainers and paddled out to join them. Matt helped her aboard, and moments later they were off.

'We're going to take a look at Great Veale,' a thin girl beside Lucy told her.

'Great Veale?'

'One of the Eastern Isles. Matt wants us to see the latest find over there.'

This was a surprise. 'He does?'

'I'm Janey Baxter. He asked me to come along because . . . well I know a bit about it, you see.' She gave a deprecating smile as if she expected Lucy to challenge her right to be there.

Lucy smiled, relieved that Janey hadn't mentioned birds, and introduced herself.

'Are you liking it up there at Polwhenna? You're in a good area for entrance graves. That's the beauty of being on higher ground. You know, of course, that the practice of communal burial may have continued much longer here than on the mainland?'

'I'm afraid I don't know much about —'

'And they think they've found some cists over on Great Veale. A new discovery, single graves. Amazing, isn't it?'

Lucy didn't think she was capable of looking as impressed as perhaps Janey expected. For one thing, she had no real idea why single graves were called cists, and wondered if by asking she would look too ignorant to qualify for a maiden trip in Matt's boat. She glanced across at him as he stood at the wheel, and he smiled back at her. Then he indicated with a nod of his head that he wanted her to move nearer to him, in the empty space beside Barbara Littlewood, which she did.

They were well out in the bay now, with a churning wake streaking out behind them. Lucy found she liked the movement and the occasional spray on her face as she leaned back in her seat.

'You're enjoying this, Lucy?' Barbara asked.

Lucy nodded. 'But I feel I'm a bit of an interloper.'

'Such a surprise, discovering Matt's new interest in archaeology. Edward has been trying to interest him in it for some time, and I've had a go once or twice but given it up as a bad job. But now . . . ' She laughed.

'So you know a lot about archaeology too?'

'Not as much as some people. But I find it fascinating that there's so much evidence on the islands that people have been living their lives here for thousands of years.'

Lucy thought about it. According to Matt, those ground-nesting birds he was protecting had been coming to the islands for as many years to lay their eggs and raise their young. Or not raise them, of course, because of an invading predator.

Barbara looked so relaxed as she sat there in her bulky jacket leaning back against the side of the boat that Lucy felt emboldened to asked her about cists.

'A cist?' Barbara said. 'An odd name

for what it is. Just an individual burial chamber. There's a cemetery of small ones just west of the Iron Age village on St Mary's. It seems these are of a later date than the entrance tombs, but still prehistoric and of great interest. But you're looking sad, my dear.'

'I was thinking of an old friend of mine,' Lucy said. 'Angus Pellow, my boss back in Truro. He would be so fascinated by all this.'

Barbara was keen to listen, and Lucy found herself telling her about her job in the bookshop that was now coming to an end. 'I shall write to Angus about this as soon as I can,' she said.

'There won't be much to see,' said Barbara. 'A bit of cleared ground, I should think at this stage, not much more.'

They were nearing one of the islands now — obviously the one they were coming to see, as they were slowing down. 'How many are keen to land?' Matt asked.

Very few of them were, but Lucy was

with them, shoes off and trouser legs rolled up to the knee. The water felt icy cold as she swung her legs overboard and followed Janey up the sandy beach. She stuck close to her as they reached the rough ground overgrown with brambles and bracken. At the top of some rising land she turned to look at *Free Spirit* waiting a little offshore. In the distance St Mary's looked hazy as a cloud passed across the sun.

Lucy tried to pick out some landmarks but saw none. For a moment she felt disorientated, as if she had come out of time and was viewing her island life as something in the past and unreachable. All of a sudden she wanted to be back on Matt's boat, with him standing within reach and smiling at her in such a way that she felt safe. But that was stupid. She was here on Great Veale for minutes only, with not much to see, as Barbara said. She had needed to find out what there was, so that she could tell Angus exactly how it looked at the present moment.

She gave herself a mental shake and then followed the others down to the beach.

12

'I gave Kevin, our local handyman, a call,' said Josh. 'He'll be round tomorrow evening and we'll have a chat about what needs doing.'

Lucy, shrugging off the jacket he had lent her, looked at him in surprise. 'Oh, you mean on Secret Haven. But it's Sunday.'

'He was glad to hear from me, as it turned out, and would have agreed to come sooner but for a job he's got over on St Martin's. He'll be finished there by tea time tomorrow.'

Janey Baxter had offered Lucy a lift up to Polwhenna. Lucy had been glad to accept, as Matt was so concerned with the mooring of *Free Spirit*. Barbara and Edward Littlewood were also concerned about her getting home. The friendship of all three was heart-warming.

Lucy had met Josh at the back door. He looked so pleased with himself for getting the work on Secret Haven organised that she smiled. 'Good for you, Josh.'

He looked pleased at her praise. 'Kevin said he'll be able to get stuck in here on Tuesday. He's a good worker. He's done work for us in the past. We've got most of what's needed, I think — paint and so on, and he keeps a lot of stuff at his place.'

Lucy hung the jacket on its hook near the front door and led the way into the kitchen. She was pleased to see that someone had wiped clean all the work surfaces, and polished them too. Not a thing was out of place.

'Great.' It was a good thing that Tanya and Annie were here, she thought. In his enthusiasm for his new project Josh seemed to have forgotten that Tuesdays were extra-busy days at Polwhenna. But she wouldn't remind him.

'Oh, and Miranda rang,' Josh said.

'She did?'

'She asked to speak to you.'

'Me?' This didn't sound good. Lucy had never spoken to Miranda on the phone before, and not often face to face either, since she had made plain her disinterest in Josh's family. 'Is . . . is she planning to come back?'

Josh shook his head. 'She has things to do. More people to see.'

'Did you tell her about Secret Haven?'

'Nothing to tell yet.'

'And did she say why she wanted to speak to me?'

Josh flicked an imaginary crumb from the draining board and then wiped his hand down the side of his shirt. 'Well no, not exactly. She didn't seem to want to tell me.'

Lucy made no comment on this. She could only think that it might have something to do with her return — but why hadn't she told Josh if that was the case? Lucy knew she had to get used to the idea, of course, and the sooner the better. But her heart sank once more at the thought of leaving Polwhenna. She took a deep breath. Maybe it would be easier if there was a definite arrangement made, instead of this vague wondering if and when it was likely to happen.

'So, Lucy,' Josh said, 'how was Matt's new boat? Did you have a good trip?'

For a moment she looked at him without really seeing him. Instead, a vision of Matt standing at the wheel filled her mind. He was so proud of his beautiful *Free Spirit*, so pleased to be taking that group on its first voyage, that his happiness was infectious. Everyone had enjoyed the experience; she could tell by the cheerful remarks and the way people were smiling at each other. She was happy too, but she couldn't help feeling a little sad at the same time. She might not have the chance to do this again, as she was committed to returning to Truro when Josh no longer needed her.

'Lucy?'

She gave a start. 'Josh — sorry. *Free Spirit* is great,' she said. 'We went to the Eastern Isles, to Great Veale. Some of us landed. Then we came back.'

This rather bald summary appeared to satisfy Josh. He gave a nod, then moved towards the kitchen. Lucy followed, trying to see the room through Miranda's eyes and failing. Nothing had changed from a few hours ago, and she didn't know how it had been when Miranda was here anyway. The corn marigolds in the blue jug Annie had placed on the windowsill between the tube of hand cream and the ceramic pot of washing-up brushes were still shedding the odd gold petal or two. There was even the faint smell of the bleach that Tanya had started to use liberally.

'Are the girls back yet?' Lucy asked.

'Making the most of their last few days on Scilly, I expect.'

'Their last few days?'

'Their time here is almost over. Had you forgotten, Lucy? They're due to move on in a week's time. I'll miss them about the place.'

Lucy would too, especially Annie and her quiet ways, which were such a contrast to Tanya's rebelliousness that struck at odd moments. She wondered if they would ever return to Scilly. If they did, she was unlikely to see them. But she pushed that thought to the back of her mind.

★   ★   ★

The holiday guests in the four cottages appeared to be getting on well together, so on Monday evening Lucy suggested an impromptu barbecue, as two of the couples would be leaving next day. This was greeted with enthusiasm. Marnie Woodcock of Tamarisk took it upon herself to organise everyone to supply food and drink, so that Lucy wasn't expected to do anything except make sure the cooking utensils were on hand.

Even Josh appeared to be enjoying himself on this balmy evening, with the smell of sizzling food rising in the quiet air. Annie had brought a box of chocolates to share, and Tanya was behind the barbecue helping Marnie dish out chicken burgers and bacon. Lucy, sitting at one of the picnic tables with a plate of cheese and salad in front of her, could just glimpse the roof of Secret Haven above the shiny leaves of a camellia bush.

Marnie's husband, Geoff, seated himself opposite her. 'You're looking a tad downcast,' he said. 'Sad to see two lots of us go?'

Lucy smiled. 'Of course. We love having you all here. The place sings when it's busy.'

'Lovely thing to say.'

'I mean it.'

'We'll come again, you know. All of us here, I think. The magic of the place gets into you.'

Lucy agreed with that. Some of the others, overhearing, joined in with their comments too. It was all good to hear, but Lucy's sadness remained. Soon it might be her last days here too, made even worse by the length of time she had been at Polwhenna. She had come to know Josh well, and to understand his deep love of the place as well as his anguish at Miranda's leaving. He was family, and she cared for him. His vulnerability had touched something deep in her, and she had done her best to motivate him to come to terms with the way things were and do something positive about the situation.

At first, seeing him begin to accept that he should be more positive had been enough reward. She had known her time here was limited, even though Angus had said she could take as long as she liked. But there were issues back in Truro that had to be resolved. She needed to help Angus dispose of their remaining stock at Good Reads, the books that he loved and were valuable to him because he thought of them as friends. She owed Angus a great deal and mustn't take advantage of his good nature. In any case, Miranda would want Josh to herself — and rightly so, if they were to build their love and trust in each other at Polwhenna again.

Lucy felt she had succeeded in what she had come to Scilly to do, but it gave her no satisfaction because she knew now that it was no longer enough. She was pleased for Matt's sake that he would in future be based here permanently, but it meant that in leaving she might not see him again.

Thoughtfully, she finished the food on her plate and then carried the empty dish back. 'Can I help with anything?' she asked Marnie Woodcock.

'Certainly not, my dear. Go and enjoy yourself.'

Lucy smiled her thanks. The proceedings were coming to an end now, and it was nice not to be involved in the clearing up. Instead of going indoors straight away, she strolled through the stone arch to the wide lawn and across to the other side of it where Secret Haven was almost hidden behind the large camellia bush, its flowers long gone. How pretty it would have looked in full bloom, she thought. She broke off one its shiny leaves and held its coolness against her face.

Tanya and Annie had spread a map of the West Country out on the kitchen table and were so engrossed that at first they didn't notice Lucy slipping in through the open doorway. Only as she filled the kettle at the sink did they see her standing there. There was such an atmosphere of excitement hovering over them that she smiled. 'Looking at anything interesting?'

'Look, Lucy — this is where we're heading next.' Annie pointed to a spot between Bristol and Bath. 'Tanya's got an aunt who lives in a place called Saltford.'

'And you'll stay with her?'

'Well, no. But she's a contact. We'll call to see her and then look for work in the area.'

'And somewhere to live?'

'No problem,' Tanya said with easy confidence.

It sounded a bit vague to Lucy, but then who was she to judge? They were young — the time to be adventurous and take what life brought up. After all, she'd come to Scilly with hardly a backward glance. She'd thought it eminently sensible at the time, though others might have thought her crazy. Angus didn't, of course. He was a dear friend. She would phone him again as soon as she got back indoors, to check how he was coping back in Truro.

Annie looked up, her face pink with excitement. 'And we've got loads of plans for the rest of our time here.'

'You have?'

'Josh says we should make the most of it.'

'Of course you should.'

'The Overlanders,' Tanya's voice was full of triumph. 'They're giving a concert on an uninhabited island next Saturday night. Menowilly, it's called. They're a local band, and they do this through the summer on different islands. We've already booked our places on one of the boats.'

Lucy smiled. 'So it'll be a late night for you.'

'And for whoever picks us up afterwards on the quay.'

'Cheeky!'

'Why don't you come with us, Lucy?' Annie said eagerly.

But Lucy declined, knowing that Josh had accepted an invitation for both of them to a meal at Sea View. Barbara Littlewood was trying out a new dish, courgette and nettle lasagne with a secret mixture of herbs and spices. Lucy was looking forward to it because she would see Rio again. The concert sounded fun, though. She thought of the boatloads of happy people going out across the water for an evening of music and laughter. And then the return in the dark across a sea she hoped would be as calm as it was this morning when she had run down to Shearwater Cove for a few moments before breakfast. The freshness of the air was invigorating, and she had disturbed a group of sandpipers enjoying themselves at the water's edge.

What would the birds of Menowilly make of the invading music-lovers next Saturday? Not much, she thought. She wondered if Matt would be going with them, but somehow doubted it. Penny, yes, but not her brother. His mind would be filled with concern for the natural life. Or maybe he would feel torn, his love of local bands clashing with his professional concerns. On the other hand, the birds might just have the sense to fly off somewhere else until they could have the island to themselves again. She imagined their leader, a rather bossy older tern, rounding them all up and telling them to take care as they flew across the water to Bryer.

'You're smiling, Lucy,' Tanya said. 'Don't you want to come with us?'

Well, did she? Lucy gave a noncommittal answer that seemed to satisfy the girls. There would be other times, she hoped. If she was still here on St Mary's, of course.

★ ★ ★

Kevin turned out to be a good worker who got stuck into things as soon as he arrived for work on Tuesday morning. Josh was there too, and they worked happily together on Secret Haven while Lucy and the girls bade farewell to the occupants of two of the cottages, then began on the preparations for the new ones who would be arriving later on the *Scillonian*. Penny called in briefly during the afternoon, and was soon deep in discussion with Tanya and Annie about the forthcoming concert. Lucy, her work done for the moment, took the opportunity to take a quick look in on Josh and Kevin, making sure that they didn't see her. They were busy finishing the floor and didn't look up. If they kept up at this pace, she thought, the place would soon be finished. It was looking good already.

She didn't stay long in case any of the new arrivals needed her for anything. Returning to the house, she made herself a coffee and carried her drink out onto the patio to sit in the sunshine.

13

Lucy stood on the darkened quay late on Saturday evening. A few others were waiting there too, and the sounds of shuffling footsteps and muted voices rose and fell in the quiet air. There was the smell of seaweed and cold stone. She shivered. In the flickering moonlight she glimpsed moving lights over on the island that was obviously Menowilly. There were bobbing lights near it on the sea too, so hopefully something was beginning to happen about conveying the concert-goers back safely to St Mary's.

She brushed strands of loose hair out of her eyes and turned slightly to give herself some shelter from the rising wind. Others were doing the same, and commenting on the time it took to get the boats away and let the dark hulk of land settle back into its normal quiet existence.

Lucy had arrived early, and was glad of the company as she waited for Tanya and Annie. Josh had offered to do taxi duty but had slumped into his favourite kitchen chair as soon as they got back from the Littlewoods, obviously totally exhausted. As the hands of the clock crept towards eleven, Lucy had left him dozing and crept out without disturbing him.

Their evening with Barbara and Edward Littlewood had been enjoyable, and the lasagne had turned out to be surprisingly delicious. Josh had accepted a second helping at once, and Barbara, pleased, had piled his plate high. It was a wonder, Lucy thought, that he'd had any room left for the chocolate bombe that followed, or for the coffee and mints. Rio had been his affectionate self and, purring loudly, followed Lucy out to the kitchen afterwards. She bent to stroke him.

'We'll leave all this till the morning,' Barbara said when Lucy had offered her help. 'I'll just deal with the leftovers.' She opened the fridge door to put the remains of the cooled lasagne inside.

Lucy smiled. 'If you say so.'

'Let's have some more coffee, shall we? And there are more mints. Up there on the shelf, Lucy, dear, if you wouldn't mind getting the tin down.'

Lucy did as she was asked, and then stood holding the tin as she spotted a small acrylic painting in a white photograph frame on the wall nearby. 'That's lovely,' she said.

'You like it?' Barbara came closer in a waft of lavender perfume to gaze at it too. 'Nice, isn't it? One of Edward's. Wishful thinking at the time he painted it. He has a vivid imagination.' Her voice was so full of pride that Lucy was charmed.

'Oh?'

'It's a Manx shearwater chick on some grass in the moonlight. Can you see the burrow behind? The little thing has just emerged, you see, and it's flapping its wings.'

'But why . . . '

'You see, dear, no one has seen a sight like that in living memory. Yet. We're hoping that this year we will. And to show how confident he is of good results, Edward painted that for me. It's hiding some rather disturbing photos from the local press.' She lifted down the picture, turned it over and removed the back. 'Here we are. Have you seen these before, Lucy? Aren't they horrific?'

Lucy wasn't quite prepared for the sight of damaged eggs and half-eaten dead chicks, made even more disturbing by being in colour. There was a tiny unrecognisable animal too, covered in blood. Speechlessly, she pointed to it.

'A Scilly shrew,' Barbara said. 'Poor little mite. The rats get some of them too, you know. They're not satisfied with trashing all the eggs and chicks; they have to attack those little creatures as well. But not anymore, we hope. Certainly not on St Agnes and Gugh, now the rats have gone.'

Lucy stared at the photos in silence.

'I haven't upset you, have I, Lucy my dear?'

Lucy shuddered. 'I knew about all this already,' she said, 'because Matt Henderson told me. About the eggs and the chicks, I mean. Not the Scilly shrew.'

'You don't often see them. Sometimes you can hear their high-pitched squeaks as they use their runs underneath the undergrowth.'

'And they'll be safe from the rats now too?'

Barbara smiled at her. 'That's the belief, anyway. They live only on Scilly, hence their name. Did Matt tell you about the one that stowed away on the *Scillonian*?'

'Really? So what happened to it?'

'Someone found it when they were about to dock in Penzance.'

'It must have been terrified.'

'All was well. It was flown back to St Mary's the next day on Skybus and released back into the wild.'

Lucy laughed. 'A happy ending.'

'But that we don't know, of course. It was a few years ago, before the rat programme got going.' Barbara was looking serious again. She collected the newspaper photos together and put them back into the frame. 'And now all this is in the past,' she said. 'No more photos like this, I hope, if the other islands remain rat-free too. But it's good to remember what it was all about, don't you think? To remind ourselves just how necessary the work has been.'

Lucy nodded. Necessary, yes, she thought now as she waited on the windy quay. Of course it was, if you wanted the Manx shearwaters' young to thrive so that the future was secure for these brave birds who flew off to winter along the coast of Brazil before flying back to lay their eggs on Scilly. And the other ground-nesting birds would be able to do this in future too, and the Scilly shrew would be safe.

There was a movement in the water now and the sound of an engine. But it wasn't a boat from Menowilly, although at first several people thought it was as it came slowly alongside the quay, its wake silver in the moonlight.

'Ahoy there, *Free Spirit!*' someone shouted.

Lucy could see Matt leaning down to pick something up. A rope. 'Here, catch this, Dave,' he called.

Dave did so and tied it expertly round a handy bollard. Lucy, keeping well back in the shadow of the harbourmaster's office, watched as Matt climbed up onto the quayside well away from where the returning boats would expect to tie up. 'I hoped I'd make it on time.'

'Too right, mate,' Dave said. 'A while yet, I reckon.'

'So what's the hold-up? I expected them back by now.'

Lucy glanced at the bobbing lights still a long way off in the distance. The sea was rougher now, and perhaps that was slowing them down.

Matt joined the group over by the steps, but Lucy stayed where she was. She still felt shaken by the photos Barbara had shown her and couldn't get them out of her mind. Matt had told her that the wildlife organisations had considered what needed to be done very carefully; had agonised over it, perhaps, before they made the decision to go ahead with the removal of the rats. The word *removal* sounded so much better than *kill*, but it meant exactly the same thing in this case. She wondered how hard the decision had been for people whose aim was to work for the good of all wildlife.

The stirring of shame she had begun to feel on seeing those horrible pictures returned now in full force. She had belittled the work Matt was doing; had refused to listen properly or to try to understand. She had let him see all too plainly that she could never sympathise with something that meant all the world to him because she believed he was totally wrong.

She glanced across at him and in the light of someone's torch saw that he looked pale. But that was the effect of the artificial light, surely? She wanted to rush to him and blurt out that she had made what now seemed the biggest mistake of her life.

But she couldn't move.

And now the boats really were coming. There was a cheer from the quay and a huge welcome as the first one approached the quay and tied up. The crowd of people on board couldn't wait to get ashore and jostled their way cheerfully onto the quay.

'It was great,' some of them enthused. 'The best one yet. Could you hear it from here?'

Lucy checked the passengers as they came up the steps, but Tanya and Annie weren't among them, and neither was Penny. By the time the fourth boat arrived she was feeling anxious. Suppose Tanya decided to stay over there for the night for one of her imaginary new experiences in which she revelled?

But there weren't so many people aboard this time, and she picked out Tanya and Penny easily as they came up the steps.

'So where's Annie?' Tanya asked when she saw Lucy standing by herself out of the shelter of the building now.

'Isn't she with you?'

Tanya looked perplexed. 'She's here somewhere. She must be.'

Most of the people had dispersed now. 'She'll have come on the first boat,' Penny said with confidence, 'and gone on ahead, got a lift with someone. You'll see.'

Cold with dismay, Lucy looked from one to the other. 'Not Annie. She'd have waited with me. I didn't see her.'

At that moment Matt came across. 'Anything wrong?'

'Annie's missing,' Tanya said indignantly. 'She hasn't come back on any of the boats.'

He looked sharply at Lucy. 'You sure?'

She nodded dumbly.

'Then I'll fetch her.

'I'll come with you,' Penny said.

'No way. Can you drive the others home, Lucy? If she's there, I'll find her, and we won't be long. I'll bring her straight across to Pengarth.'

In moments he was down the steps and into his boat, calling out to Penny to untie the rope and throw it to him. The engine springing to life sounded like thunder.

★   ★   ★

Afterwards, Lucy couldn't remember driving Penny home and then Tanya. All she knew was that all three of them were tense and silent as she drew up outside Pengarth. The lights downstairs were on, and as Penny got to the door it opened and she was drawn inside.

When Lucy pulled up and parked back at Polwhenna, all was in darkness. Tanya, seated beside her, was shivering. Lucy felt cold too, and suddenly weary.

Suppose Matt couldn't find Annie — what would he do then? Come back without her and alert the rescue services, who wouldn't be able to do anything until first light? At what stage would they contact Annie's parents in Australia? The horror of it all was overwhelming. And they still had to tell Josh.

They got out of the car and a light in one of the front windows flicked on. Lucy, opening the front door and feeling for the light switch, saw at once that Tanya looked dreadful. Her hair was damp and she had pushed it back behind her ears. Her jacket was done up on the wrong buttons, giving her a ragged look.

'It's my fault,' Tanya said in a trembling voice that didn't sound like her at all. 'You see, I thought she was on another boat.'

'Stop it, Tanya. How can it be your fault? Matt will find her. Don't worry.' But how could she help it? Lucy thought. Of course she was worried, just as she was herself.

The sitting room door opened and Josh emerged, yawning. 'Sorry, Lucy; I must have dropped off. Where's Annie?'

The phone rang. Lucy and Tanya jumped, but Josh strode calmly towards it and picked up the receiver. 'Hi, Matt. You're what? Oh, I see. Yes, Lucy will be there, or I will. See you!'

'Are they all right? Both of them?' Lucy's mouth felt dry.

Josh looked vague. 'Matt said he's on his way back to Pengarth Beach, that's all.'

'Nothing more?'

'You'll have to put me in the picture as we go, Lucy. I promised Matt we'd be there to meet him.'

'And Annie?' Tanya whispered. She grabbed Lucy's arm. 'I'll come too.'

Lucy shrugged her off. 'No way. You need to get warm. It's cold out there. Make some soup to have ready. Fill some hot water bottles. Do something useful.'

Josh nodded at her. 'Do as Lucy says, Tanya.'

For a moment she hesitated. Then she shrugged and pulled off her jacket. 'Don't be long then.'

Lucy smiled in relief. She had expected argument but to her surprise had got none.

At Pengarth, Josh parked as near to the beach as they could get and left the headlights on as guidance for the boat that was still out there somewhere. It was a wonder that Penny or her parents hadn't heard them arrive, Lucy thought as she scrambled out. She considered alerting them, but then thought better of it. Matt would tell them what happened soon enough, and before that all they could do was wait.

They shaded their eyes so they could pick out the tiny flicker of light that must surely be *Free Spirit*. Josh said little at first. He had made no comment on the situation, and Lucy hadn't speculated either on the reason for Annie being left behind. It was made clear on the booking form that people must be responsible for themselves. She wondered if anything like this had even happed before.

'So we wait,' Josh said, his voice quiet.

The light from the moon faded as a cloud passed across it, and then it was bright again. The dancing waves, higher than before, now seemed threatening with their silver highlights dipping wildly from one minute to the next. 'Conditions were like this when Miranda left,' Josh said. His voice was even quieter now, and Lucy had to strain to hear him.

'They were?'

'Daytime though, of course. It wouldn't have seemed so bad.'

'I suppose not.'

'It was her eyes, you see. She thought she was losing her sight. She wanted to see someone in London, someone she knew.'

'She told you this?'

'She told Matt's parents. They

211

thought I should know, you see. They told me the night of their barbecue.'

'Ah. So why didn't you . . . ?' Lucy began and then stopped, confused.

'Why didn't I tell you?'

It wasn't what Lucy was going to say, but she didn't tell him that she was about to question his lack of action or indeed concern for the wife he professed to love. In Josh-like fashion, he had just let things slide. But this wasn't the moment to confront him with that.

'But it wasn't the reason she didn't come back,' he said.

'Oh?'

'She wanted more from me and I wasn't sure I could give it. She believed Polwhenna meant nothing to me; that I didn't care what happened to it or to her.'

'She said that?'

Josh shuffled his feet. 'Not exactly.'

'Then why . . . ?'

He didn't say anything for a moment, and Lucy, watching him closely, saw a nervous tic at the side of his mouth.

'Is that what you think Miranda believes?' Lucy said.

'It must be true.'

'Why should it be true?'

'Just look at me, Lucy. What good am I to her, a lovely woman like that? She's talented and beautiful and funny. She could have chosen anyone.'

'But she chose you, Josh.'

'And made the mistake of her life.'

'Did she tell you that?'

'Well no, not in so many words. But I let things slide. Polwhenna was near to closing down.'

'But not anymore. Not now, Josh. It's thriving.'

'Due to you, Lucy. You've made me see what I had to do.'

'And you've done it.'

'You think so?'

She knew that of course, but did Miranda? He could be utterly maddening at times, and this was definitely one of them. 'But have you told her that?'

'I think so?'

'You *think* so?'

'In any case it's too late now.'

'Too late?'

'She's flying here from Newquay on the early plane tomorrow.'

14

Lucy's room at the back of the house seemed different this morning. For a moment, on waking, she lay and wondered why this should be. Then she remembered: Matt was here, sleeping in the spare room on the floor beneath hers. Warmth crept round her heart at the thought.

Then the events of last evening came rushing back and she felt again the cold horror of discovering that Annie wasn't with the returning concert-goers; that she was still over there somewhere on a dark uninhabited island, abandoned, and wasn't answering her phone. How scared she must have been as she watched the lights on the boats fading away into the distance.

But Matt had leapt to action, and it was because of him that Annie was safe at Polwhenna now. She hadn't thanked him. No one had.

Then Lucy registered, suddenly, that the wind had dropped, and instead of the fierce conditions of the night before there was this stultifying silence. She sat up and looked at her bedside clock. Just after five a.m.! It wasn't only the shock of the news that Josh had come out with last night that had woken her so early, as she had thought at first. It was this odd silence. A pearly light blotted out the branches of the holly tree outside her window. Could you be woken by deep silence? she wondered. It was such a contrast to the sound of the heaving sea and the fierce wind last night when *Free Spirit* finally got back and Matt had come in as far as he dared before he dropped anchor. He was over the side at once and lifting Annie out to carry her the short distance to shore.

Their relief at seeing her had been enormous. 'Is she all right?' Josh called out.

Matt put her down. 'Nothing to

worry about, thank goodness. Warmth and food would be welcome. But she's all right. She just missed the boat, that's all.'

He made it sound like merely missing a bus, but in the gleam of the car headlights Lucy could see the lines of concern at the corners of his mouth and the way his arm was supporting Annie. Lucy ran to her.

'My ankle,' Annie murmured.

'It's injured again?'

'I twisted it but it's all right now. I thought it was broken. I couldn't get back to the beach at first. Then it was too late. I didn't know what to do.' Her voice broke on a sob.

'But you're OK,' Lucy said to reassure her. 'We'll get you home as quickly as we can. It's all right, Annie.'

There wasn't time for more, because Josh was insisting that Matt come back with them to Polwhenna for the night. There was a spare room, unlike at Pengarth at this time in the holiday season, and immediate sustenance on hand too if Tanya had got the soup ready. It was simpler to take Matt with them than let him drive himself back in his wet state to his friend's small place near the quay.

Now Lucy leapt out of bed and reached for her clothes. There was a lot to do today. Two of the properties would be vacated by about ten o'clock and must be made ready for their new occupants. Annie, she suspected, might be too traumatised by her night's adventure to be capable of doing much. It was too early yet to go and check on her, but she would do that at the first opportunity. And then, of course, Miranda would be arriving at Polwhenna, expecting all of Josh's attention.

Downstairs, the kitchen was the untidiest Lucy had ever seen it, and today of all days this wasn't good. Last night they had all been glad of Tanya's sweet potato soup and of the vast quantities of buttered toast she made as they were eating it. But at well after midnight, they weren't going to start on the washing-up or putting anything away in its rightful place. Lucy had made up the spare room bed for Matt and then downed the coffee Josh made for her and headed for bed. Her cousin had found some of his spare clothes for Matt after his shower, but she hadn't waited for the two of them to finish their meal. She had thought she wouldn't sleep, but she was wrong.

Now she collected together the china and cutlery they had used last night and ran hot water in the sink. The house was unusually silent at this hour. By now there was birdsong outside and the whispering movement of the pittosporum branches against the wall. The mist was clearing a little, though, and she could see the courtyard wall and the holly tree on the other side of it. She wondered if the planes would be flying in this poor visibility. A worrying time for the visitors who should be leaving, as well as for the new ones. And Miranda, too. What would she do if she was stranded on the mainland?

Lucy's few memories of her included Miranda's impatience on her wedding day when the car booked to take the bride and groom to the station in Penzance had been five minutes late.

There was the sound of a door opening now, and Lucy spun round, her hands dripping water as she lifted them from the sink. 'Matt?'

He grinned. 'Don't sound so surprised. Had you forgotten I was here?'

As if she would do that! She felt sudden warmth in her cheeks. 'You're up early, that's all.'

He hooked a chair out from beneath the table and sat down. He was wearing a grey sweatshirt and long brown shorts that on Josh looked as if he had just thrown on the first things that came to hand. On Matt they looked good. His dark auburn hair was slightly rumpled though, and he was wearing an old pair of flip-flops on his feet that Lucy recognised from the wicker basket Josh kept near the front door.

'Will I do?'

She smiled as she returned to the washing up. 'Why wouldn't you?' She lifted a last plate out of the bowl and placed it carefully in the rack. Without looking at him, she said carefully, 'We're so grateful to you, Matt. Thank goodness you were there. It would have terrible if — '

'I was there. Full stop. Penny wanted to be met, so I was there in the boat to take her home. Don't dwell on what might have happened, Lucy, just on what did.'

'I wish I was that sensible.' She shuddered. She didn't want to think about what might have happened if Matt hadn't acted so swiftly, but she couldn't help it.

His expression was full if sympathy. 'I know — your imagination is running riot. But just think of this, Lucy. There was no problem on the other side. Annie came hobbling down towards me at once when I got to shore, happy to see me. She'd been huddled up in the shelter of the sand dunes, very sensibly, having lost her mobile phone.'

'But she thought no one would come for her until the morning.'

'Until she saw the lights on *Free Spirit*.'

'I'll get that kettle on,' Lucy said. She dried her hands on the towel. She should have thought of tea or coffee straight away.

'Tea please,' Matt said as if she had asked. 'Any more of that soup left?'

'Sorry. How about scrambled egg instead?'

'Perfect. But you might have to do a lot. I heard sounds of movement as I came downstairs.'

She was glad to have something useful to do, and got out a packet of bacon too. Even though she wanted to raise the subject of the bird protection programme, she knew there wouldn't be enough time on their own if they were soon to be interrupted. In any case, Matt might think that her gratitude to him for his rescue of Annie was the reason for coming out with her sudden change of heart.

Josh, when he came into the kitchen a moment or two later, seemed even more preoccupied than usual, although he commented on the smell of sizzling bacon that met him. By this time, Matt had found the cutlery and laid places for five.

'A bit optimistic?' Lucy said.

'Who knows,' he said, 'but I'm looking on the bright side. Those girls might surprise you yet.'

At that moment, the sun came out of the rapidly thinning mist and flooded the kitchen in golden light. Lucy dished out bacon and scrambled egg for three. 'Josh?' she said.

'Oh. Thanks.'

He sat blinking on the sunny side of the table, and Lucy pulled down the blinds a little before she sat down herself and helped herself to a large chunk of the bread that Matt had been cutting. They ate in silence until Matt finished his and pushed his chair back.

'That was good, Lucy. Many thanks.

And now I must be off.'

Lucy looked up. 'I'll drive you to collect your car at Pengarth.'

'No need. I'll walk.'

'In that footwear?'

He glanced down at his feet as if surprised to see what he was wearing, and she smiled at the expression on his face. His trainers were still wet, so it was no use to think of wearing those. 'I'll manage,' he said.

Lucy had no doubt he would, and she knew it would be no use arguing. With thanks again for the meal, Matt was off.

* * *

Josh left for the airport at three o'clock and Lucy heard the plane come in fifteen minutes later. But it was well after half past four by the time she heard the rattle of the car drawing up outside. She had time to wonder at the delay. Maybe Miranda had changed her mind after all or not shown up at the right time.

The new people for Tamarisk had arrived earlier than the specified arrival time of two o'clock, but their place was ready for them and it posed no problems. In fact, Lucy was glad to see them, because welcoming them and showing them round filled in some of the waiting-for-Miranda time. And yes, they could use the pool straightaway if they liked. Lucy wished she could dive in too, to relax and rid herself of some of the tension she was feeling as the time of Miranda's arrival approached.

The other family hadn't come yet, but they could show up at any minute; and since the girls weren't here, Lucy needed to be on hand. Both Tanya and Annie had got up late, which she had expected. Tanya came running downstairs full of energy; but it was Annie, following close behind, and who seemed no worse for last evening's adventures, who was the surprise.

Lucy marvelled at her energy as the three of them set about their cleaning rota. Only sometimes did she catch a glimpse of something in Annie's eyes that hinted at some fresh knowledge she had gained of herself. No one knows how they would react in certain situations, Lucy thought, until they experience them at first hand. Annie had accepted that no one would come for her until first light and had acted sensibly. She had already told Lucy that the place she had found in the dunes provided shelter from the wind and had felt quite safe.

'We were all spread out along the beach, you see,' she had said. 'And when the boats were loading, everyone made a dash for them.'

'But not you?' Lucy had said.

'I tripped and fell. I called out but no one heard. My ankle hurt. I couldn't walk on it, but then it got better.'

Lucy had thought of the lost phone but didn't remind her of it.

At least three planes had gone out by now, and the sun was shining. They had a quick lunch of bread, salad and cheese out on the patio, and then Lucy suggested that Tanya and Annie had done enough work for the day and were free to make the most of the rest of it. She smiled at the speed they took themselves off.

Now, waiting for the new arrivals and for the sound of Josh's car returning with Miranda, Lucy wandered across the lawn to take a quick look at Secret Haven, at the same time listening for the sound of car engines. The door had had a coat of fresh white paint, and someone had cleaned the windows. She peered through and saw that the wooden flooring had been finished to a high standard, and the walls looked far better than before, as they were now pale primrose-yellow. No furniture yet, of course, but Josh had told her that wouldn't be a problem. There was plenty stored in two of the top-floor rooms in the house; Josh was merely waiting for Miranda to make her choice of the most suitable pieces.

Lucky Miranda, Lucy thought now.

It was the sort of job that anyone would like, putting the finishing touches to a job well done. She turned away to go back indoors, stopping to smell the honeysuckle in the courtyard for a moment and regretting that she had always been too busy to appreciate everything to the full. But then she realised that her upcoming departure from Scilly and return to the mainland was casting a gloom over her thoughts. Of course she had appreciated everything. She was down at Shearwater Cove so often that she almost felt she lived down there. She loved the curving stretch of silvery-gold beach and the island that wasn't always an island, there to be explored at low tide. Matt had promised that they would do this together one evening when conditions were right. Had he forgotten? She certainly hadn't, and thought of it often when she was on the brink of sleep.

It was on the beach that she had spent those magical moments with Matt the first evening. They had walked round to the other, smaller beach, and he had talked to her of the work he was involved in and how much it meant to him. She wished now she had listened more sympathetically and at least tried to understand the importance of it, which she had come to realise now, at last. The dull ache in her heart was hard to bear.

She went in through the kitchen and into the hall, which still smelt slightly of lavender from the polish Tanya had applied to the telephone table rather too liberally. She stopped for a moment to wipe a smear off the edge, then looked thoughtfully into the looking glass above it. Her face looked paler than usual and her hair limp. She pushed it back behind her ears, but the result was not pleasing. What had happened to her in the last week or two, she wondered, that made her seem so exhausted?

The sound of a car driving up and stopping made Lucy pause in her thoughts for an instant. A taxi, or Josh's car? She ran to open the front door.

15

Matt parked his car behind the town hall in a designated parking space. He hoped it wasn't too early for Janey Baxter to be up and about. She owed him a favour, as she made sure to remind him every time they met, her forehead creased with worry because she hated being beholden to anyone. Well, now was payoff time, he would tell her. With pleasure, he would watch her expression brighten as she gave one of her rare smiles.

He got out of his car and pulled out the bag of wet clothes. He'd had a hard enough job convincing Lucy that he would deal with them himself, and felt a sense of achievement as he walked the short distance to Janey's door in the row of terraced stone cottages. She opened it at once, as if she had been waiting for him.

'I have a job for you, Janey,' he said. 'I had a bit of a swim last night.'

Her eyes opened in horror and he hastened to explain. She seemed more worried about his wet clothes than about poor Annie left marooned on Menowilly, but he assumed that would kick in later when she had had time to reflect. 'I'd be grateful if you'd put them through the machine for me,' he said. 'I've got some work to do in the office this morning. I'll call in for them later.'

Matt handed over the bag and was smiling too as he left her and walked back to the car. But he hesitated. It was still very early, and a breath of sea air wouldn't come amiss. Porthcressa Beach was always one of his favourites, perhaps because his mother had liked to rest there after shopping when he was small and he had happy memories of making harbours among the boulders to one side of it when the tide was out.

It was in today, though, tiny wavelets

teasing the ragged lines of brown seaweed washed in overnight. Matt walked slowly along the promenade. Sunlight sparkled on the sea far out and the air smelt salty. There always seemed to be more bird life here than at Pengarth, and he recognised the screeching cry of herring gulls and the muted call of a distant tern. He thought he caught the thin reedy sound of a shearwater but couldn't be sure.

He seated himself on a seat in a sheltered curve of the wall that already felt warm. As he stretched his legs out in front of him he was aware, suddenly, of the shabby flip-flops on his feet and that he'd forgotten to collect his soaked trainers from the back door of Polwhenna. But no matter. No one was expected in the office today, and in any case his feet would be out of sight beneath his desk. He was in no mood for small talk about last evening's events when there was serious stuff to consider about the proposed trip to Menowilly tomorrow morning by a history group from the mainland. It seemed that they were doing a project on Victorian life on the islands and were keen to see for themselves some of the ruined cottages and locate the graves of that time. They might or might not be aware that this was the terns' breeding season. The obvious thing to do, of course, was to take a trip over there himself to be on hand.

A vision of Lucy's concerned face in the light from the car headlights flooded his mind. Annie, relieved not to have been abandoned after all, had been unconcerned by the loss of her mobile phone, but Lucy had been anxious. He might even do a bit of searching for it tomorrow, and suggest to her that she might like to come with him to help find it.

He leapt up and strode purposely back the way he had come, anxious now to get going on the report on a new group of volunteers that he wanted to get done by Saturday morning.

'Something wrong?' Tanya asked when she and Annie appeared at the kitchen door as Lucy was about to serve the chicken casserole she had put in the oven earlier for the four of them.

Lucy made an effort to look cheerful. She had been making a huge effort to be delighted to welcome Miranda, and had planned on making her favourite meal — according to Josh, a mushroom and courgette lasagne — even though Tanya considered it poison and would want a separate meal. And yet Miranda hadn't arrived.

Josh had shrugged in resignation as he came indoors and wiped his feet on the doormat far longer than was strictly necessary. He muttered something about Miranda having arranged for a taxi to meet them to take her and a friend to Penmarrow Guesthouse in Ennis Street.

'But why?' Lucy had asked.

'She's anxious about him. She wants

to see him settled in.'

Josh was struggling to sound as if that was reasonable, but Lucy could that he was under a great deal of stress. And no wonder. But she said no more, not wanting to make things worse for him at this stage.

Now she smiled at Tanya and Annie and asked if they had been doing anything interesting that afternoon. In all the chatter, Josh's low spirits went unnoticed by them. While the girls were washing up, Lucy suggested Josh come for a walk with her down to the beach and up to Carn Head for some exercise, and to clear his head a little. It would also be a chance to talk to her if that was what he wanted.

He shook his head. 'Things to do.'

'Really?'

'Matt will need his trainers. I need to see him anyway.'

'Then we'll head in that direction.'

'One of us should stay here in case we're needed.'

Lucy hesitated. She saw Josh glance

quickly at Annie and away again. So that was it — he felt his responsibilities keenly after last evening. She didn't know what he imagined might happen, but she took his point and nodded.

★   ★   ★

With her eyes closed, Lucy was reclining on one of the sunbeds she had brought round to their private court-yard. The distant cooing of a wood pigeon and the faint scent of bruised grass seemed to lull her senses into a dreamy state in the cool of this lovely evening. A peaceful time like this was unusual enough for her to revel in it with pleasure. A bumblebee hummed nearby, and there was the sound of distant birdsong.

But after a while thoughts of Josh began to intrude. It wasn't surprising that he wanted to deal with the latest development on his own, but Lucy wished he wouldn't always push her away when she wanted to help. Perhaps the two-mile walk to Matt's temporary home in Hugh Town would help him a little.

Several moments passed before something so obvious struck her that she wondered how it hadn't occurred to her before. He was planning to accost Miranda and her male friend at Penmarrow Guesthouse!

No, surely not. But Josh had been different lately, more assertive, and Lucy had been glad to see it. His efforts to complete the work on Secret Haven with a view to a long let to someone who would also act as caretaker at Polwhenna on occasion were admirable. And so was the way he stood for no nonsense from Tanya when she was in one of her moods.

Now that the idea had occurred to her, Lucy couldn't rest. She could imagine only too well what might happen when Josh turned up: a nasty scene not appreciated by the owner of a guesthouse with other guests looking on.

She sat up and swung her legs over the side of the sunbed. But what could she do about it? Phone the guesthouse to warn them? Phone Matt and ask him to rush to Ennis Street to intercede? She took a deep breath. It could be that her imagination was running away with her. She sprang up and went indoors, through the kitchen and into the hall, where to her relief she saw that Matt's trainers were no longer where they had been left for him to collect. But Josh's mobile phone was on the telephone table, where he often left it, so she couldn't phone him to discover his intentions. Good and bad.

The front door handle rattled. For a second or two Lucy stared at the door, so immersed in her suspicions she couldn't move.

* * *

'So tell me,' Miranda said, 'where that dreamy husband of mine has got to? Don't tell me he's off on some scheme of his own that doesn't involve Pol-whenna?'

She sounded so pleased and interested that Lucy looked at her in surprise. They were seated at the kitchen table, and Lucy had produced glasses of ice water, which was all Miranda would accept. Lucy still felt dazed by seeing her so unexpectedly, uncertain of how to cope with her cousin's estranged wife turning up looking as if she had stepped out of a fashion magazine. Her make-up was flawless, and her fair hair was swept back into a chignon that set off the elegance of her cream silk blouse and slim-line skirt to perfection.

Lucy raised her glass to her lips and then put it down again. She felt at a distinct disadvantage in her T-shirt and shorts. But why should she? Miranda was the one looking out of place. Miranda was the one who had taken it upon herself to make life difficult for someone Lucy cared about. She wasn't going to be brow-beaten by anyone, and certainly not by this woman. 'Josh is returning some lost property,' she said.

Miranda appeared not to be listening. She was gazing round the room, her brow furrowed. Then she raised one leg and contemplated her strappy sandal for a long moment. Sitting up straight again, she looked at Lucy with resolve. 'He's too fixated on this place to the exclusion of everything else.'

'But he thought he should be concentrating on Polwhenna; that you believed he'd lost interest in it. That's why he's been working so hard on — '

Miranda raised one perfect eyebrow. 'He thought that?'

Lucy said nothing. This was their business, Josh and Miranda's. It would soon be obvious that all four cottages were occupied and the booking chart healthy.

'He muttered something about Secret Haven,' Miranda said, 'when I saw him at the airport. I didn't quite catch on. There were other things to think about and our taxi was waiting.

I'll need to inspect the place to see if it's suitable.'

'Suitable?'

'There's someone interested in taking it.'

Lucy didn't want to get involved with that at the moment. She drank the rest of her water and placed her empty glass away from her so she could rest her elbows on the table. 'Then you should inspect it for yourself, Miranda. I'll get the key for you. Then I've a phone call to make. I shall be busy for the next fifteen minutes, so please bring the key back with you. I'll see you then.' She stood up.

★ ★ ★

Matt answered his mobile at once. 'Yes, Josh has been here, and my trainers have been delivered. But where he is now I've no idea. Is it important?'

Lucy explained about Miranda turning up and wanting to see him. Then, making up her mind suddenly, confided her anxiety about a confrontation between her cousin and the man Miranda had brought back with her.

To her dismay Matt laughed. 'I don't think that's at all likely, Lucy. And you wouldn't either, if you saw him.'

She would have to take his word for it, but she wasn't happy. There were voices outside now. 'It's all right, Matt,' she said with some relief. 'I'll have to go.' She clicked off and thrust her mobile in her pocket.

Josh and Miranda were outside the front door and their voices sounded friendly. Lucy heard Mirada's light laugh and Josh's responding words. She ran to the kitchen, shut the door and leaned against it, thinking hard. Tanya and Annie weren't expected back for ages, and she herself was definitely in the way. She could escape with ease and spend the rest of the evening down on the beach and neither of them would notice her absence. The space and freedom down there were appealing. Suppose that phone call she made to

Matt was the last time they spoke?

The thought of that wouldn't allow her to lie motionless on the soft sand and contemplate the peaceful scene before her with any pleasure when she should be drinking it in. So she walked down through the ragged lines of dark seaweed to the mass of rounded boulders that joined Carn Island to the beach and were visible at low tide. They were unbelievably difficult to clamber over, and she had to concentrate hard to keep her balance because of their rounded shape. Every now and again she stopped to look at the view of the Eastern Isles, hazy in the evening light. The sea was as smooth as a silk sheet, and she felt a magical quality in the pure air.

At last she climbed onto rough turf almost covered by brambles and growing bracken, but there was a narrow path of sorts that took her up to the higher land. Here she was totally alone, she knew, because the only approach was the way she had come, and she would know at once if she was being followed.

She walked further, pushing her way through the undergrowth, until she came to a bank that looked as if it could have been man-made perhaps in prehistoric times. Angus would know. She would do a bit of research on that when she got back.

She found a spot to sit where she had a fine view over to Shearwater Beach, where the whole expanse of silvery sand was bright in the evening air, although the marram grass behind it and the low bushes and overhanging pittosporum were encased in shadow.

How could she bear to leave all this and return to her old life?

She forced herself to think ahead, to make plans to get online to the steamship company, check train times from Penzance, contact Angus and her neighbour, pack. Plenty to do, and she would do some of it tomorrow and get things moving so she was out of Josh and Miranda's way. Tanya and Annie would be moving on too, and she could be available for driving them to the airport or to the quay. She hadn't asked them about their plans for leaving the island, but she would do so as soon as she saw them.

Lucy thought of Miranda in her lovely clothes. Josh had sounded so happy that it brought tears to her eyes now, and she wiped them away with the back of her hand.

And saw Matt.

It could be no one else striding across the sand like that. He shaded his eyes, then waved. He had seen her.

She stood up. He made short work of the boulders she had found so difficult and was with her a few minutes later. 'Lucy!'

Her heart quickened as he took her in his arms. 'You knew I was here?' She leaned against him, and when she raised her face he bent and kissed her.

'You cut me off on the phone,' he said. 'I didn't know . . . '

'Miranda . . . '

He kissed her again, and this time she allowed herself the joy of knowing he had come to find her; that he didn't want to lose her. She felt his warmth and his quickened heartbeat and knew that nothing else mattered but this precious moment.

'Ah yes, Miranda,' he murmured at last as he stood back. His expression was tender, and Lucy marvelled at the suddenness of this. She was hardly aware of anything but the slight breeze on her face and the nearness of someone who meant the world to her.

'I'll have to leave the island now,' she said.

'You'll come back?'

Of course she would. Sometime. Somehow. Miranda had seemed different — softer, more friendly — but that meant nothing. There was no reason to suppose that Lucy would be welcomed to Polwhenna. But Matt had asked her to come back one day, and so she would.

'Will you come with me tomorrow in

Free Spirit?' Matt said. 'I need to go across to Menowilly. The Victorian history group is going there.'

'But isn't it prehistoric Scilly you're interested in?'

'Well yes.' He hesitated. 'It's . . . it's the birds, the terns. It's their nesting period and they mustn't be disturbed.'

'And you think the group will go rampaging all over the place, trampling on the eggs and young chicks?' Lucy's eyes danced at him.

'I'll keep a look-out, that's all.'

'Then I'll be glad to go with you and help look out for them. Will we have to fight off the rats too? And what do we do if we find evidence of them, apply poison in tubes? I hope we'll take some with us.'

'You'd help me do that, Lucy?'

His gaze was so eloquent she shivered, aware that this was a moment of great significance. She raised her eyes to his. 'I would, Matt.'

He took her hands in his. She knew he could say no more for a few wonderful moments in which he strove to keep his composure, and she gladly gave him that time.

At last he smiled. 'I was afraid to mention my purpose for going over there. I was going to mention the lost mobile as my main reason.'

'That too,' Lucy said, smiling now. 'We'll do that. Three things.'

'The history group wants an early start,' he said, 'taking advantage of the state of the tide. So we'll go tomorrow early, you and me. The terns should be fine after last night's activities over there, but you never know.'

She thought of something. 'Penny — will she be going too?'

His eyes shone as he smiled. 'Not on this occasion. But come on, Lucy — let's get ourselves back to the beach before it's too late.'

The tide was beginning to come in now, very gently stirring the seaweed. The way back was easier because Matt held Lucy's hand, and the strength in it was reassuring. Once on the soft sand, he took her in his arms again.

'There's so much to talk about and plan, Lucy. But I know one thing: I want you by my side for the rest of my life.'

His words were heart-warming, and she walked with him up the steep track to Polwhenna in a hazy dream in which there was no tomorrow, only this glorious present.

* * *

Matt was at the kitchen door the next morning before Josh and Miranda had surfaced. Only Tanya was at the kitchen table, eating fruit and fibre cereal as if her life depended on it. She and Annie planned to be busy today, squashing their belongings into the two bags each they had brought with them.

Lucy scribbled a reminder note about where she was going and pinned it to the noticeboard for the others to see. They were so involved with their own plans that they might easily have forgotten what she had told them when she'd got back the previous evening.

Matt's car wasn't outside as Lucy expected, and he smiled at the expression on her face. 'We're heading for the beach here today,' he said. 'I came round by sea and I've borrowed the family's rubber dinghy. No paddling out in cold water for us today.'

She smiled too, and they set off hand in hand down the track to the beach. The foxgloves on the bank seemed to stand up more proudly, and the red campion looked more startlingly pink than she had ever noticed before.

A little way offshore, *Free Spirit* was at anchor. Matt helped Lucy into the dinghy, took the oars and they were off. Moments later they were aboard, the dinghy attached to the stern and the anchor stowed in a safe place.

The sun burst forth from a hazy cloud as they set out, highlighting one island and then another. The distant beach on St Martin's was a sheet of gold. Some shags skimmed the water, and Lucy saw a couple of cormorants on a rocky outcrop. Behind them, St Mary's receded into the morning mist.

Matt's hair brightened in the strengthening sunshine. Lucy's heart was too full for speech, and he said nothing either, but he looked supremely happy. All too soon, Menowilly was close, and Matt slowed the engine and then cut it off. He reached for the anchor and threw it overboard. Lucy watched it descend through the twinkling water and settle on the sandy bottom.

A few moments later, they were on the beach with the dinghy pulled up above the water line. A little way off another boat was anchored, larger than *Free Spirit*.

Matt removed his jacket and threw it into the dinghy, and Lucy did the same with hers. Then he took her in his arms and kissed her. 'We haven't long,' he murmured. 'We need to check on the nesting sites.'

'Of course.'

They climbed the hill, pushing their way up through the bracken to the top on a path so hidden it was almost invisible.

'This and the other paths will be cut back later on when the nesting season is over,' Matt said. 'But we can manage, I think. I'll be able to gauge the tern situation from the top here and check that the historians are nowhere near them.'

He plodded on ahead without waiting for Lucy's answer. She had been searching the ground as they walked for a glimpse of Annie's mobile, but she could see it was unlikely the girl had come up here when the action was down on the beach.

Matt raised his binoculars to his eyes and nodded in satisfaction. 'All seems well,' he said as he handed them to Lucy. 'There's a group of people over there, but they're well away from the nesting sites.'

To her ignorant eyes there was little else to see. A few birds were flying about, but that was all. She was pleased that Matt was happy and handed the binoculars back to him with a smile.

They went down another way to a different area of the beach, and Lucy spotted Annie's mobile at once among some marram grass. She picked it up and rubbed some loose sand away. 'Annie will be pleased.'

'Is it OK?'

'I'll try it and see.' She tapped in the phone number of the house phone at Polwhenna, listened for a few moments and shrugged. 'No answer. I'll try Josh's mobile.'

He answered after the first ring. His voice sounded more upbeat than she had heard for a long time. 'That's good,' he said when she had explained her mission. 'Miranda's got some good news too, Lucy. She's found a possible tenant for Secret Haven who'd be happy to do some caretaking duties when needed. We've arranged a viewing of the place tomorrow. Isn't that great? He's staying down in Hugh

Town at Penmarrow.'

'You've met him?' She was surprised. Could he possibly be the man who had accompanied Miranda to St Mary's?

'Briefly,' he said.

'And?'

'A nice chap. He's looking forward to meeting you, Lucy. I thought — '

The line went dead. Lucy clicked it off and put it in her pocket. 'The battery's run out.'

'Come here,' Matt muttered in a low voice. The sun was warm on her back as he held her close. He pulled her down beside him on the sand and she closed her eyes. Breathing in the smell of his skin as he kissed her was wonderful, but soon the group of historians would be back, unaware of this magical moment that would live in Lucy's mind forever.

She was the first to break away, smiling at her sentimental thoughts. Matt sat up too. 'They're here?' he said.

'I can hear voices.'

He held out his hands to pull her too her feet, his eyes full of amusement. 'A group of Victorians would be shocked at our behaviour.'

'You think so?'

'Well perhaps not this lot.'

They were coming now, laughing and chatting, looking anything but staid in their bright holiday wear. But the dark trousers and jacket of one person were in stark contrast to the shorts and T-shirts of the people around him.

Lucy was astonished. '*Angus?*'

He smiled as he saw her. 'Lucy, my dear.'

She rushed to him and then turned to see Matt at her side. He seemed to size the situation up immediately, and there was hardly any need for introductions. All the same, she explained the basics to Matt, her words tumbling over each other.

According to Angus, Miranda had called in at Good Reads in search of a suitable book on archaeology for Josh, and they had got talking. One thing led to another, and here he was, having made the decision to sell up at last.

'And Miranda made you decide that?' Lucy said in astonishment.

'She's a persuasive lady. She'll have that husband of hers immersed in prehistory before you know it.'

Lucy's laugh was a little shaky. There was a lot to take in, and there wasn't much time to do it, because the leader of the group was looking at his watch. 'So what are you doing over here today, Angus?' she said.

'Today we're looking at the remains of buildings and suchlike from the Driver Survey.' Angus spoke as if he was one of the society already, and Lucy hid a smile.

'And all the prehistoric stuff?'

'That's for another day.'

'There's masses of it.'

He gave her a sweet smile. 'I shall have plenty of time for that, my dear. I think I've made up my mind already to settle here on Scilly.'

The leader was urging them to make haste, as the boatman was anxious to be off. Lucy watched them go, standing beside Matt on the wide expanse of sand. The teasing breeze was stirring it into little white eddies now. She brushed her hair out of her eyes.

'We'll have plenty of time, too,' Matt said. 'All our future. But I think this is the right moment for us to leave here too. What do you say to that, my love?'

Lucy thought about it, and then a rush of joy engulfed her. She would go with him gladly, anywhere he wanted to go. Well, she would if that was where she wanted to go too.

She smiled up at him. 'Have I any choice if I don't want to be marooned like Annie?'

'All the choice in the world, my love, as long as it's the same as mine.'

'Shearwater Cove,' they said in unison. And laughed.